Our City of Light

G H Rehling

The Conrad Press

Our City of Light
Published by The Conrad Press in the United Kingdom
2024
Tel: +44(0)1227 472 874
www.theconradpress.com
info@theconradpress.com
ISBN 978-1-916966-55-0
Copyright © G.H Rehling 2024
All rights reserved.
Typesetting and Cover Design by: Levellers
The Conrad Press logo was designed by Maria Priestley.
Printed and bound in Great Britain by Clays Ltd,
Elcograf S.p.A.
All the characters in this novel are fictitious.

1

Heedless of our season of havoc, summer had come early to Paris that year. The slow green waters of the Seine glittered turquoise in the sunlight and fresh young leaves danced in the playful breezes that skipped between the plane trees. And I would gaze upon these things and remember my father, who could delight in the brilliance of a summer's day yet hold in mind the night to come.

I used to think of my father often in those days, just a year since his death – the smell of cigar smoke and expensive cologne, the sharp suits and vivid buttonholes; the lightness of his wit and the weight of his wisdom. Here and now we enjoy the light of day, he would say, but we must never forget that, there across the horizon and there in the shadows, darkness waits, and it will have its turn. No fervent prayer nor Talmudic disputation has yet prevented the world from turning, nor the dark from overtaking the light. Do you see?

Did I see? Did I really see? Not at first, not even when they came for me that Monday – the 10th of June, 1940.

After the long drawn-out exertions of the Perrenoud case, I had been awarded a day off and, from a bitter-sweet combination of exhaustion and desire, I spent it in bed with Ammarah. I was dozing by her side, the fingers of one hand interlaced with hers, the other resting on the warm, gentle slope of her naked belly. But as I drifted and dreamed, drawn towards the source on tides of merciful forgetfulness, I seemed suddenly to hear the sound of distant drums. The beat of the drums loomed closer and closer, quickening and insistent like the pulse

of one suddenly in peril, like the harbinger of some atavistic dread.

I found myself seated on the edge of the bed, sweating and shaking my befuddled head. Ammarah was pushing me in the back with her feet.

'Go on, you idle devil, answer it. It's your door, Joseph, if you haven't forgotten.'

Her feet were cold despite the suffocating summer heat that lay across the city, and I made some feeble joke about it as I wrapped my late father's silk dressing-gown around me and stood for a moment, watching her, admiring her.

'All right, I'm coming,' I yelled as the pounding on the apartment door resumed.

In the absence of my family, the array of closed doors in the sunless hall seemed to oppress my spirits, and brought suddenly to mind the forlorn landings of La Santé prison, where François Perrenoud awaited justice for the kidnapping and murder of a Jewish businessman, Adolphe Cohen. Only the door to the drawing room stood ajar, offering a glimpse of the gleaming grand piano at which I had suffered uncounted excruciating hours of childhood.

'Just coming,' I assured my callers.

I opened the door to an ill-assorted pair of guardians of the peace. One too young, fresh of face and eager – if he'd been equipped with a tail it would have been wagging – and his companion much too old, panting and sweating from the climb. Neither of them looked as though he would know how to use the newly-issued carbine hanging from his shoulder. We stood in silence for a moment, the neophyte staring expectantly into the face of his aged companion, who continued to gaze imperturbably into the middle distance like the statue of Serenity.

'Inspector Simon?' the youngster ventured at last.

4

'You have tracked me to my lair,' I replied, immediately regretting my levity when I saw the kid blush with chagrin.

The older man roused himself from his reverie to come to the lad's assistance.

'You are wanted, Monsieur Inspector, at Saint-Paul Métro station. Commissaire Roland says he will meet you at the scene.' The words creaked their way through the white soup-strainer moustache in a cracked falsetto, the accent that of the Midi.

'The scene of what?'

'Murder, sir,' said the kid, unable to contain himself.

'You'd better come in while I put some clothes on.'

Tucking their shiny new helmets respectfully under their arms, they stepped into the hall and, at my invitation, sat in the chairs on either side of the low table on which my father used to keep magazines – La Vie Parisienne, Paris Match, Jazz Hot and Marie Claire – for his waiting patients, an eclectic selection of Paris society. Now it was occupied by an Art Deco bronze of a female dancer, nude, cast in the implausible act of reaching to catch hold of the crescent moon. My mother was widely admired for her 'eye'.

'What are your names?' I asked, partly to distract their attention from the embarrassing object.

'Peres,' panted the older man, who looked relieved to be seated, 'and this young fellow is Picard.'

I nodded and smiled in acknowledgement as I cautiously opened my bedroom door, careful to block their view since, last seen, Ammarah had been entirely uncovered on the bed. But now she was fully dressed and seated at the dressing table, about to apply the scarlet lipstick that complemented so alluringly the rich coffee tones of her skin.

'I heard,' she said. 'I'm on at nine, so I'll be away now.'

5

She turned her head so that I might kiss her, which I did, greedily.

'Look after yourself, lover boy,' she whispered, her soft breath in my ear like a surge of electricity running through my being.

I gazed out of the window to watch her going. The street was quiet in the still, bright daylight. There was only the tiny figure of Madame Maurer, the concierge, sweeping some dog mess into the gutter.

Dogs were everywhere in those days, abandoned by their fleeing owners to wander the streets alone, and the authorities were beginning to fret for fear that the poor bereft creatures might transmit rabies, or that they might become feral and form ravenous, child-eating packs. Such fearful fancies ran through the streets of Paris and the corridors of power hourly – terrifying and titillating in equal measure, and far more dangerous than any poor starving mutt on the lookout for a meal and a friendly face.

Ammarah stepped into the street and, guessing that I would be watching, turned to wave and blow a kiss up to me. I watched until she was out of sight and then, sighing, I turned my gaze upon the open wardrobe.

However urgent the call, one must dress to meet it and, if there is time to dress, there is time to dress with care. From my wardrobe I selected the lightweight brown suit with its wide lapels and rich cream stripe, a cornflower-blue shirt with a soft collar, and a dazzling silk tie of my father's in blue and sunshine gold. I may have mentioned that he was quite a dandy, a Parisian flâneur of the first order, the old man. I seized his Panama hat from a peg as I passed through the hall, carrying the two men in uniform in my wake.

2

A small crowd of onlookers had gathered at the entrance of the station, but their curiosity seemed somehow to lack commitment and energy, as though they were merely going through the motions of some ghoulish obligation. Priorities were bound to change, I supposed, when the audible menagerie of gunfire – grumble, woof, whine and squeal – was drawing closer every day and the enemy was rattling the gates of your city.

The wealthy had already fled, for the most part, but the poor, especially the Jewish poor – and this remarkably silent crowd was predominantly Jewish – had nowhere else to be, so they might as well be here in Place Saint-Paul, looking on and doing their best to savour the latest sensation. Idly surveying the crowd, I remembered that the square had once been known colloquially as Place des Juifs, Jewry Square, sitting, as it does, at the heart of the Pletzl.

Turning back to my escorts, I felt a sudden, obscure unease, a sense that something else – beside the bloodlust of the mob – was missing from the picture; and then I had it.

'No press?' I remarked to Peres, who appeared to nibble somewhat at his moustache while he considered this unprecedented state of affairs before answering with a slow shake of the head.

'Next to no newspapers,' he said simply.

So, no importunate arseholes pushing through the crowd straight at you as though you owed them a favour. No pencils poised to record the inspector's every banal observation, ever hopeful of a career-busting indiscretion or the unintentional confession of a blunder. No attention-seeking shouts, no blinding lightbulb flashes nor metallic magnesium stink.

No, just a bunch of rather cowed looking women in pinafores and house coats, and old men – white beards, black Homburgs – and a plume of blue, funereal smoke rising from the old men's cheap cigarettes and hovering in the still air above them like fate.

'Is it true, inspector?' one of the women called.

I looked back – a redhead, about forty, a little heavy around the hips but still something about her.

'Is what true?'

'That the Germans have massacred everyone on the train? That they're camped at the Château de Vincennes? That they're about to invade the city by Métro?'

I shook my head in disbelief and started down the steps, taking Peres with me and leaving young Picard to join the officer on guard. The familiar base note of the Métro system – armpits, burnt grease and scorched rubber, stale urine – rose to meet us as we made our way down to the platform and I pumped the old boy for information.

He and Picard had been the first police officers to arrive on the scene, having been intercepted by the breathless ticket-collector from the station as they crossed the square on a routine patrol. Public telephones had been cut off, so Peres had to send his young companion running to the nearest police post for help, while he accompanied the distraught railman to the first-class carriage on the recently arrived train. He gave orders to secure the scene as best he could – three passengers had alighted from second-class cars and had already left the platform before the body was discovered – and went to check the victim.

'You did well,' I said.

He stopped on the stairs and touched my sleeve to bring me round to face him.

'I've not seen the like since my young days in Marseille, monsieur inspector; not since the Corsicans and the Italians were at it, monsieur,' he said. 'And the face...' He shook his head slowly, the white moustache drooping as though it had been let in on some dark existential secret.

'What have we got about the people who've left the scene?'

He stopped to consult his notebook.

'There was an elderly couple, the Bronsteins, off the rear carriage. The ticket collector knows them well because they go every Monday to see their daughter in the sanatorium – consumption, poor thing...'

'Yes, well, I doubt they'll make the list of suspects. Who else?'

'A young man in a fair old hurry, according to the ticket collector. The flower-seller upstairs remembers him too, running out of the station and across the square in the direction of the river.'

'Description?'

'Young, black suit and hat... That's all we've got. No one took much notice at the time.'

We reached the platform at last and there he was, somehow at the scene before me. Commissaire Arthur Roland, Gargantua in a peasant's Sunday suit, notebook lodged in one mighty fist while he questioned a group of people at the far end of the stranded train, pausing every now and then to lick the tip of his pencil in an act of elephantine delicacy.

'Them that found the body,' said Peres, squinting at them in the feeble electric light – half of the bulbs having been removed to conserve power – 'and that's Commissaire Roland himself,' he confided in awe.

9

Within the Paris prefecture, it was common to refer to Roland as 'Maigret' – indeed, I often heard it vehemently maintained that he was the sole model for Simenon's fictional detective – but it was an epithet never used to his face lest he took it the wrong way. Older hands were always quick to remind the youngsters that, in his rugby-playing days, he had been nicknamed Le Bourreau, the executioner.

The commissaire raised a hand to acknowledge my arrival, and waved me in the direction of the first-class carriage. The faces of forsaken second-class passengers stared out at us as we passed, some distressed and tearful, some resigned, some clearly seething with impatience to get on, checking their watches and huffing in exasperation. Uniformed officers moved among them, checking papers, taking details, vainly seeking someone who might admit to having seen something.

We reached the rear door of the first-class carriage – the middle of five cars, red to distinguish it from the green of second-class – where another uniformed officer stood guard.

'Right,' I said to Peres, taking out my notebook, 'for the record, what have we here?'

'The body of a male, aged about thirty, found at 19.02 by boarding passengers...'

'Boarding first-class? At Saint-Paul? The Rothschilds visiting, were they?'

He ignored my flippant interjection and pressed on.

'Stabbed. No one got out of first-class here, and there was no one else in the carriage.'

Respect to the old man – he might have a spot of senile tremor in his voice but he knew the essential facts when he saw them. So I asked him another.

'Who will be the juge d'instruction?'

Was there the slightest involuntary twitch of a smile beneath those walrus whiskers?

'The examining magistrate? That will be Monsieur Leclerc, sir.'

'Oh, fuck!' I couldn't help it.

With Leclerc on the case the demands for minutely detailed documentation, for the triplicated justification of our every thought or action, would be never-ending. One of his foibles was an unshakeable confidence in his unique acuity in the forensic analysis of crime scenes. Pity the poor dumb police officer who 'trampled all over' the scene of a crime before the omniscient Leclerc had made his examination.

I had committed this error once and had no intention of revisiting that humiliation on my own initiative, so I waited for my superior to join me.

I did not have long to wait. The key witnesses – 'Them that found the body' – were considerately shepherded past me by a lugubrious agent de police, no doubt on their way to 36, where we would later take their depositions.

I watched them attentively: a short, stout gentleman in a frock coat and high hat, alternately consoling a drooping young brunette of undeniably lavish proportions, and complaining at being inconvenienced in this way; a hatless young man in a brown suit, and his brisk but pretty girl, both of whom seemed unusually composed in the circumstances; and a bewildered couple of about thirty, the husband carrying a sagging cardboard suitcase, his Homburg riding high on his head as though it intended, at any moment, to leap off and dash for cover. Refugees, I reckoned – Jewish, surely.

Now Commissaire Roland was striding towards me. He must have been well into his late forties or even fifty – who would dare ask? – but his movements betrayed no loss of physical assurance. He retained the shoulder-rolling swagger of an athlete, his chin thrust forward like

11

the prow of a battleship beneath a broad forehead topped with cropped salt-and-pepper hair. A pork-pie hat sat square on his head, absurdly out of proportion, and he wore a stub of pencil behind the ear in the manner of a joiner. But the overwhelming impression was always that of the sheer size of the man; the height, the breadth, the imposing fact of him.

'Right,' he said, gesturing to the uniformed officer on guard to open the door, 'let's get to it.'

3

'Shouldn't we wait for the juge d'instruction?' I suggested nervously, following him into the carriage.

'Not coming,' he said, squeezing his way along the aisle. 'Phoned me. Sending over a commission rogatoire.'

I whistled. 'Leclerc? Dishing out a warrant to carry out your own investigation in your own way, without constant reference to him? Why, boss?'

'Questions, questions,' he mumbled, coming to a halt in order to view the scene from the perpetrator's perspective. 'Getting ready to run from the city, like the rest of the rich and the powerful, I expect. No one left in my building but me and my wife.'

For a policeman, Roland inhabited an improbably spacious apartment in an unfeasibly grand building in rue Brunel, just off the Boulevard de la Grande Armée – a gift from the late president of Stade Français Rugby Club to his legendary captain.

'Look. Think. Seen the like of this before?' he said, nodding in the direction of the victim.

Our man sat on the thin leather cushions of the front seat in the attitude of one who had fallen into a doze on his daily commute. Any casual glance in his direction would make nothing more of him, and I wondered how many stations he had sat through without anyone noticing the tiny wound, a single spot of blood at the base of his skull.

The commonplace instrument of his murder had been left on the seat behind him, the wooden haft worn smooth by a thousand hands, the slender length of steel coming to a point. An ice-pick – one in every middle-class home, and every bar, café and restaurant in Paris. This must have been a swift and precise execution, the blade angled to drive up into the base of the brain. One blow, instant death.

'Laetitia Toureaux, back in '37, perhaps?' I suggested, recalling one of the first cases I had worked on – the pity, the frustration, the failure. 'But this is no defenceless young woman, this looks like a big man, able to look after himself.'

'So the killer must have been very sure of himself – if he got within striking distance, he knew he wouldn't fail. He's done it before, or he's been trained to do it.' Roland had stepped in front of the victim. Suddenly he crouched, looking up into the face. 'My God! Will you look at this, Jojo?'

Leaning in to peer into the victim's face, I gasped involuntarily. The facial features were all but burned away. It was as though someone had carefully arranged layers of rumpled cobweb across the face, so that one might discern the features as generically human, but distantly, vaguely. A frosted glass phial – the kind of vessel one might find in a laboratory or a pharmacy – had been placed between the feet, so that it wouldn't rattle around.

The trousers were eaten away above the knee and in the groin, and the raw meat of the thigh muscle was exposed as though it had been subjected to anatomical dissection. A pool of whatever corrosive fluid had performed this macabre work of art had formed on the floor, and an astringent vapour hung in the air, making breathing a painful ordeal.

As one, we stood and retreated a short distance, examining the scene.

'That's a decent bit of tailoring he's wearing,' Roland observed, as though to turn his mind from the image of that face.

'London cut, I reckon,' I agreed, joining him in the flight from horror. 'My father once... Very expensive,' I gabbled, suddenly not wishing to draw attention to my cossetted origins.

The suit was navy blue with a discreet stripe, the shirt was white with a soft collar, the knitted tie was red to match the faint line in the worsted. A brown fedora rested on the seat beside the body.

'The hat looks top drawer too,' I added. 'English again, I should think.'

Roland reached across the corpse and plucked the hat from the seat, turning it over so that we might read the label, Lock & Co, St. James's Street.

'So, do we have an Englishman?' Roland wondered aloud. 'Or a Frenchman with expensive tastes and the cash to feed them? Or something else altogether,' he mused, tapping his teeth with his pencil.

'Not necessarily English. There's a shop called Le Savile Row on the Place Vendôme, where you can find English tailoring. My father went there once, but then he felt guilty about it, I think,' I ended sheepishly, before moving on hastily, 'Shall I go through his pockets now?'

'No, let the photographer at him before we move anything,' said Roland, deftly replacing the hat on the seat. 'Hold on a moment, what's this?'

He pointed to a golden pinhead on the left lapel. With his pencil he turned the lapel until we saw a little golden badge concealed on its reverse. Leaning closer, holding my breath against the acrid fumes, I could see that the badge bore a tiny enamelled crucifix, the letters 'CDFC' running across it. We frowned at each other.

Finally, Roland shook his head, 'No. You?'

I shook my head in turn, 'No, boss, means nothing to me either.'

The commissaire drew himself erect and called down the carriage, 'Right, let's have the snapper in here, double quick.'

The police photographer was a meagre, sharp-featured little fellow who wore his sandy hair long in the attempt to conceal a receding hairline, and whom no one had ever seen without a cigarette jutting from a corner of his mouth. In one hand he carried a collapsible tripod, and in the other a camera the size of a man's head.

'All right, Lapaix, get on with it,' said Roland, standing back to allow man and machine to pass.

As the photographer drew a tape measure from his pocket and began to set up his shots, Roland and I ceded him the scene and went to stand on the platform.

'Right,' said Roland, clamping one enormous hand on my shoulder. 'Two questions: what kind of man would have the skill, the knowledge and the nerve to do this? And why are they so keen to wipe out the identity of the victim?'

'Military training?' I ventured.

'I had military training,' he said, 'and it didn't involve learning to spike a man's brain like a laboratory frog – more your general purpose bayonetting in the guts.'

He paused, suddenly faraway, as though remembering.

'Still,' I said, 'could be some sort of commando operation – a German advance party, fifth columnists...'

The shops and streets of Paris, the offices of the police, the meeting-rooms in the ministries, all were aflame with fear and rumour – a fifth column of armed traitors in the city, an imminent communist insurrection, German paratroopers landing in the Bois de Boulogne; German paratroopers disguised as policemen, German paratroopers in nuns' habits. On it went, building by the hour, a delirious fever whose crisis had not yet come. And now I was at it.

'The Germans, eh?' said Roland, fully recovered. 'The Germans are about to overrun the city, so they kill one man – with an ice-pick – throw acid or something in his face and send him through Paris on the Métro? Well, remind me to bear it in mind.'

'Could be political though? The communists, the fascists, the anarchists? The acid on the face could be an extra grisly touch – humiliation, erasure – a warning to others not to break ranks. Or, more obviously, an attempt to conceal his identity.'

Roland nodded thoughtfully, 'Or criminal gangs. The Algerians, the Italians maybe, or our very own bad boys – drugs, women, guns, gambling, protection... Our man obviously had money, and plenty of it. I think we can be fairly confident it's not a domestic row about whose turn it was to put the cat out.'

The photographer slunk past us, resembling a dockside pimp in the Breton cap he now affected, and we re-entered the carriage. The dead man's pockets yielded little of interest – a wallet containing 970 francs, a pink first-class Métro ticket, a clean, neatly folded handkerchief, and the carnet from which the used ticket had been torn, eight tickets left. No identity card. Nothing, in fact, that offered any clue to his identity.

'Who goes around without ID these days, with random checks at any moment?' said Roland, waving a massive hand in the direction of the victim's devastated face. 'I don't believe it. You're right, Jojo, this man was deliberately stripped of his identity after he was killed, and giving it back to him is going to be the key to finding his killer. We've got the tickets – so where were the

17

tickets with these serial numbers sold, and who bought them?'

4

Back at 36 Quai des Orfèvres, the commissaire decreed that we would be taking witness statements together in his office. One glance through the smoke-bronzed window of 'the aquarium', the office I shared with two other inspectors, one of them still a probationer, and I could have wept with gratitude.

Clément was sprawled in his chair with his stinking, shoeless feet on the desk, puffing away on his odious bonfire of a pipe and scratching at his crotch like a mangy baboon, while young Nevin, having just spotted the chief in the corridor, was frantically shuffling papers and flicking through index cards, as if to prove that he was entirely unaware of the presence of a walking legend, and was carrying on exactly as usual. I raised a hand in greeting but neither responded.

Gratefully, I followed the commissaire to his office. He went straight to his chair, leaving me to deal with the light-switch. In the instant before the light flickered on, I heard the pitiful creak of the chair as he lowered his bulk into it.

In the unlikely event that an early anchorite had been offered a view of Roland's room from his lonely eremitic cell, he would have smiled and nodded in rigorous approval of its austerity. There was a sturdy desk of maple wood bearing only a leather-framed blotter and a telephone receiver, behind which Roland balanced uncomfortably on his long-suffering swivel-chair, rather in the manner of a rhinoceros at last mastering the art of riding a unicycle.

In front of the desk there were two cheap plywood chairs of the kind one might find in a synagogue soup kitchen and, behind them, a book-case stocked mainly with out-dated police manuals and unread policy directives. Just inside the door stood an old-fashioned hat stand of dark wood from which two coats hung almost to the floor: a belted raincoat and a winter overcoat fashioned from what might well have been an old blanket. A grey metal filing cabinet sat immediately behind Roland and to his right. I had never seen it opened.

The walls, in institutional cream, were entirely unadorned – no mementos of a glorious career in club and international rugby hung there, none of the various certificates of commendation that I knew he had earned in his time with the PJ, and no indicators of any allegiance whatever; not even a family photograph. The window offered a consoling view over the Seine and the Left Bank, and its broad sill was my favourite perch in the commissaire's office.

We took our witnesses in the order in which they had appeared on the crime scene. According to the conductor, the body was discovered by 'the fat bloke with the top hat and his bird,' so we started with them. He was a – or, by his estimation, the – Monsieur Julien de Nouailles, a senior functionary in the Ministry of Finance.

After a preamble in which our witness established that he was first cousin to no less a personage than the Duc d'Ayen, that he was a chevalier of the Légion d'Honneur in recognition of his long and distinguished record of service to the Republic and that, worse still, he was a near neighbour and frequent dinner guest of Monsieur Mandel, the Minister of the Interior, the commissaire brought him abruptly to the matter of the murdered man on the Métro.

Roland's brusqueness and transparent lack of interest in his honours and social standing seemed to puncture the man's self-importance, and he became suddenly compliant, obsequious even, and clearly anxious to get away. A film of sweat gleamed on the dome of his bald head and formed glistening drops on his upper lip, and he kept consulting a gold pocket watch as though time might be about to catch him out with some sudden and capricious leap forward or back.

His girl, Mademoiselle Louise Reski, was in her early twenties, round-faced with a long straight nose, full ruby lips and moist brown eyes. She wore a wide-brimmed hat trimmed with silk violets, and a single red rose adorned her impressive décolletage. She sat at a little distance from her gentleman friend, her gloved hands clasping a small morocco bag and her eyes demurely downcast. Unless prompted, she seemed content for him to speak for both of them.

It seemed that Monsieur de Nouailles had reserved a table for two at Maxim's at 7.30, so he had finished work a little early and made his way to the Reski family's apartment in Hôtel de Bergerac, rue François Miron, arriving at 6.45pm. After a brief but cordial exchange with her parents, Monsieur de Nouailles and Mademoiselle Reski had walked directly to Saint-Paul to take the Métro to Concorde. On boarding the first-class carriage, she saw it immediately.

'Saw what, mademoiselle?' Roland turned to the young woman, insisting on specificity.

'That poor man.' Tears started to flow.

Her lover, sighing with embarrassment or impatience, checked his watch again. Time proceeded at its normal pace. Roland leaned across to provide her with a neatly pressed handkerchief.

'That horrible little hole at the back of his neck.'

'I knew at once that the fellow was dead,' said de Nouailles. 'I've seen enough corpses in my time.'

The young woman's plump cheeks quivered as she regarded him with eyes suddenly wide with fright.

'You served in the last lot, monsieur?' Roland asked, one veteran to another.

'Of course. You, Commissaire?' Roland inclined his head to the slightest degree. 'Verdun?' Roland's head nodded twice.

'Ah well, you know then.'

There was suddenly a warmth of understanding between them.

'What did you do then, after you'd found the body?' Roland asked.

'I screamed,' said the woman. 'It's silly, I know, but I couldn't help it.'

'Not at all,' Roland and de Nouailles said in chivalrous unison.

'Did it bring help – your scream?' I asked, smiling at her.

'It did indeed,' her lover replied. 'The young couple came running from the next carriage. He said he was a doctor.'

'Dr Henri Caron and his fiancée, Mademoiselle Thérèse Gilbert, a nurse at the Salpêtrière,' said Roland, consulting his notebook.

'And then the other pair,' de Nouailles continued disdainfully, 'with the suitcase. I have no idea what they thought they could offer.'

'Aid to someone in distress, perhaps?' Roland suggested.

The other man flushed, checked his watch again, 'And then the conductor, of course.'

The telephone at Roland's elbow suddenly jangled, and our witnesses both started as though an electric current had been passed through their seats. She subsided with a nervous titter as Roland picked up the handset, and her lover, eyes narrowed, glanced at her before checking his watch yet again.

Roland spoke briefly into the telephone, listened, spoke again before covering the mouthpiece with his hand in order to address the witnesses.

'Apologies, I must take this. But, before I do, there is one last thing. Were you on the platform as the train came in?' They nodded. 'Did anyone get out of the first-class carriage before you got on?'

No one, they were certain of it.

5

I returned from showing our witnesses back to the waiting-room to find Roland concluding his conversation on the telephone.

'That would be good, Monsieur le Préfet. If you'd have it sent to me, for my eyes only, first thing... Thank you again.'

He looked up at me as he set the receiver down, the burden of the ages suddenly upon his shoulders, yet something exultant in his eyes.

'That was Monsieur Langeron, the prefect of police. He's had the minister, our man's dinner chum, onto him – we're to send him and his playmate home straight away. De Nouailles is needed, apparently.'

So we moved onto the second couple on the scene – Dr Henri Caron and Mademoiselle Thérèse Gilbert, the hatless young man in the brown suit and his neat, brisk little fiancée, both blond and blue-eyed, rather stereotypically Teutonic in appearance. As Nevin hustled them into the commissaire's office I noticed something that had escaped me on the Métro platform – the young doctor limped, lame in his left leg, and wore a bulky, clumsy-looking boot on that foot.

'Talipes equinovarus,' he said, seeing that I had noticed and, to gloss the medical jargon, 'Club foot. It's why I'm still in Paris, and not working in a field hospital at the front.' He shrugged, smiling faintly, 'I knew it would be good for something one day.'

He joked more in resignation than bitterness, it seemed to me.

They appeared a quiet, pale sort of couple, but they had had the guts to run to the aid of a screaming woman, not knowing what they were walking into, when most people sat tight and looked away.

'Dr Henri Caron? Mademoiselle Thérèse Gilbert?' Roland said, shuffling their identity cards on the desk before him.

They nodded and he turned to the note which Nevin had introduced into the room with them.

'The Salpêtrière acknowledges you, you'll be glad to hear. What is it you do there again, doctor?'

'I'm just an intern in neurology.'

'That's not what it says here,' said Roland sternly, causing the doctor to frown and his companion to flush with anger.

She had neat features, too regular to strike one as beautiful, in a small face framed by fair hair which she let down, I imagined, only when she was off-duty.

'Here it says that you're the best neurology intern they can remember. What do you say to that?'

It was the young man's turn to blush, as his woman gripped his arm and shot him a look full of pride.

'They said that?'

'The professor himself...'

'Well, he's never said it to me,' the young man said with a self-deprecating laugh, flushed with pride and delight.

'You had a good look at the body, doctor?'

He nodded.

'What would you say was the cause of death, doctor?' Roland's voice had acquired a slightly threatening, aggressive edge.

'A narrow-bladed instrument thrust between the first and second vertebrae, through the foramen magnum and into the brainstem. I found an ice-pick on the floor a few rows back – it must have rolled there with the movement of the train...'

He noticed Roland frowning.

'Death would have been instantaneous,' he concluded limply.

'A man would have to know what he was doing.'

The doctor thought for a moment, contemplating his joined hands, the thumbs resting on his chin.

'I suppose he would. Without knowledge of the anatomy...virtually impossible. For this to result from a chance blow, a stab in the dark, as it were, well... the odds against such a thing would be unimaginable.'

'A doctor would know the anatomy, wouldn't he, doctor? Especially a neurologist.'

The young man looked up, startled, paler than ever. Roland regarded him sternly, his gaze fixed on the young man's face.

'So it was you who placed the ice-pick on the seat, was it? Why did you pick it up, monsieur?'

'I... I know that was a mistake, Monsieur le Commissaire. One should leave forensic evidence where it lies, but I was rattled, I'll admit it, as shocked as anyone there and... it was a reflex, like something one does in a dream... random, unconsidered...'

'Not to account for your fingerprints being on it then?'

'This is ridiculous!' the young woman cried, her pale eyes blazing with icy light as she regarded Roland with contempt. 'Henri did nothing...'

'But try to help, I know,' said Roland. 'Still, you must consider yourself a person of interest in the inquiry, doctor. Just a formality, really, but no leaving Paris without our clearance.'

'Where would I go?'

For the rest, their story was simple and credible enough. After work, they had walked from their attic apartment at 12 rue Villiot to catch the Métro at Gare de Lyon, intending to alight at Concorde and walk back through the Tuileries and then beside the Seine, enjoying what might be one of their last fine summer evenings of freedom. It sounded like a good plan, the sort of thing that young lovers should do.

As he was dismissed the young doctor suddenly smirked ironically.

'You know what they – other doctors – say about neurologists, don't you?' We waited for the answer. 'They say we're very good at putting a name to the problem, but useless when it comes to doing anything about it.'

6

This left only the refugee couple, Alfred and Miriam Lederer. The hare-eyed probationer, Nevin, hurled them into the office along with another of his notes to Roland, and bolted as though the commissaire, given time for a more measured appraisal, might decide that he'd make a tasty snack.

Though worn down by the disease of poverty, the Lederers were a handsome couple.

She was too thin and cruelly strained by hardship, but a dauntless beauty shone through the dark, observant eyes and in the coils of glossy black hair that spilled from the cage of a little round hat which bore a single brave feather – pheasant, I thought. Her dress was black, as though she was in mourning, but around her neck she wore a loosely-knotted silk scarf, defiant in its gem-like, floral brightness. As I have found often to be the case, the woman seemed to have starved herself so that her man might thrive.

He was a big fellow, tall and well-muscled, and he held her to him as though he feared that she might be swept away from his side by the inexorable tides of history. He wore a decent enough blue suit, just a little on the turn by the look of the slightly frayed cuffs and the shine at the elbows, and maintained an implacable grip on the shabby suitcase which probably contained all that they had in the world.

As he folded himself into the offered seat, he thought for a moment before electing to balance the suitcase on his knees and his ill-fitting Homburg on top of the suitcase.

Roland watched them as they settled into their chairs – she drawing hers as close as possible to her husband's – while he mounted reading glasses on the upper slopes of his nose in order to read Nevin's note. Eventually, he gave a grunt of satisfaction, ripped the reading glasses from his face, and addressed the witnesses directly.

'In your own words, what happened and what did you see?'

The woman spoke for both of them, often glancing at her husband.

'We have been offered jobs and a room at a restaurant in rue des Hospitalières-Saint-Gervais, and were on our way there. We caught a train at the Porte de Vincennes and got off at Saint-Paul and, as we walked along the platform, we passed the front door of the first-class car and saw that there was a disturbance.'

A 'disturbance' – she spoke French slowly and precisely, carefully placing all the correct parts of speech into their correct positions, as though she were assembling some intricate and dangerous mechanism.

'Your French is very good,' Roland remarked.

'Thank you, but it is slow, I know.' She looked exhausted, dark rings beneath her eyes. 'One of the ladies I worked for, she was a teacher, she helped me a lot.'

'You have been working?'

She looked alarmed, as though she had walked unknowingly into a trap.

'Only waiting on tables, cleaning a few places, and cooking for a nice elderly lady...'

Roland raised a hand to reassure her that he was not interested in that.

'You could have walked on but you didn't, you went into the carriage. Why?'

She shrugged, 'It is true that we do not want trouble, to be involved with the police, you know. We are stateless people now, and it is best not to draw attention, but we could not just pass by – in case there was something we could do. But there was not.' She finished with a sigh, 'He was dead, stabbed in the head, I think. Someone had found an ice-pick on the floor.'

'An ice-pick? Your recognised it as an ice-pick?'

'Of course. My family have... had a restaurant in Teplice-Šanov. We used them all the time. And, I told you, I have been working as a waitress sometimes here in Paris, too.'

Roland looked towards the husband, one eyebrow raised, seeking some contribution to their account of what they had seen and heard. Seeing this, she spoke for him.

'My husband does not speak French yet. He understands and can read a little, on signs and the like.'

'What is your own language?'

'Czech or German. We are from Teplice-Šanov where most people speak German, but we are Czech...and Jewish.'

'Do you and your husband speak Yiddish?' I interposed.

She coloured. 'Sometimes, a little.' I understood – Yiddish for their more intimate conversations.

Seeking permission with a glance at the commissaire, I leaned across the desk and spoke to the husband in Yiddish, calling him Mr Lederer and then Alfred. He spoke freely, looking often and solicitously at his woman, and expressing his relief and gratitude at being enabled to lift some of the burden from her by working at last. He confirmed the details in his wife's statement and then, with my encouragement, recounted their own history.

When the Germans invaded their homeland, their restaurant – a Jewish family business – had been subjected to such harsh restrictions that it could not remain in business under their ownership, he said. They had decided they must flee the country and had sold the restaurant for a pittance to a local German-speaker and new-minted member of the Nazi Party.

By the summer of '39, they had made their way by degrees to Paris, where, so long as he remained jobless, their only home would be a cabin built of dismembered crates and scavenged corrugated iron in the zone, near the Porte de Vincennes. Now they had, at last, the chance to make a new start; jobs and a clean, dry room at Rozenstroikh's restaurant in the Pletzl.

'In a Jewish, family-run restaurant in a city that's about to be taken by the Nazis? I'm sorry,' I said pitilessly, conscious mainly of my own predicament.

'They will not dare to behave that way in France, in Paris,' Madame Lederer asserted, also in Yiddish, but the pallor of her face betrayed less confidence than her words.

Roland looked at me questioningly.

I shrugged, 'It checks out, boss.'

'Fine, he said, shoving some papers across the desk to them. 'Your cartes d'étrangers look fine, but they'll need updating with your new address. Take them to the mairie of the 4th in the morning – if anyone's still working there. And Nevin's checked with the restaurant,' he said to me. 'The job and the room are confirmed – all kosher.'

I laughed and even the witnesses smiled at his little joke. He looked pleased with himself as he sent them on their way with apologies and good wishes. From the window of the commissaire's office, I watched them disappear into the thickening darkness, hand in hand like the babes in the wood.

31

Behind me, Roland noisily cleared his throat. 'We need to find that running man,' he said.

7

It was approaching midnight when I left 36 to walk home. In the blacked-out streets every journey on foot was like a venture into an unknown city full of hidden perils. One could easily sprain one's ankle in a hole where a cobble should be, or stumble over a dog snoozing on the warm pavement, or collide head-on with a fellow nightbird as one rounded a corner.

The residual heat of the day radiated from the stones of the city and the night air seemed to have an unhealthy, feverish quality, causing me to break out in a sweat. I paused to take a breath and light a cigarette on the parvis of the Hôtel de Ville and made it to rue du Renard without incident, following in the footsteps of my younger self, who had run home from school this way a thousand times. No, more than that, I thought, calculating; far more than a thousand.

I found myself remembering the day that my parents had moved the family here, beyond the unmarked bounds of the Pletzl but within a ten minute stroll of the bakeries and restaurants that they loved – more precisely, that my father could not bear to leave behind forever, or indeed for more than a day or two – and would continue to patronise.

My parents might have risen in the world, professionally and socially, but the move to Rue du Cloître Saint-Merri was no step up. Rather, it was a shuffle sideways, just beyond the tight circle within which everyone knew everybody else's business and eyebrows were raised at my mother – the daughter of a popular reformist rabbi – and her family's persistent truancy from shul on the sabbath.

So we were to live one foot in and one foot out – feeling ourselves to be fully French, if not always accepted as such, and fully Jewish though we practised no religion.

By then, my father could have relocated us to a more prosperous and reputable district. Somewhere with trees, where ladies in furs walked with little dogs tucked beneath their arms. Instead, he moved us just around the corner from that seat of erotic infamy, rue Brise-Miche, where the working girls used to delight in turning my pallid cheeks bright red with their remarks on my person, their sudden caws of mirth, and their 'special' (and very specific) offers. I loved it, right from the start.

I turned into rue du Cloître Saint-Merri and walked into a dazzling carnival of light. Bright electric light shone shamelessly from second floor windows and spilled across the narrow street, where a sombre streetlamp stood in spot lit and inflexible reproach, as though on a stage set for the unfolding of dark deeds and retribution.

The windows of the Simon salon were flung wide to the night, and there was music too – a drawling female voice, jaunty brass, American, unfamiliar. Even though I was unable to make out the words, the plangent sound moved me and made the hairs on the back of my neck stand up.

Despite the late hour, Mme Maurer stood, all metre and a half of her, at her open door, leaning on her broom.

'Ha, Monsieur Joseph, I'm glad to see you back at last,' she said. 'Poor Mademoiselle Soubry...'

I didn't wait to hear any more, but raced up the stairs two at a time, heart pounding with anxiety.

She was swaying gently to the music, her back to the door, a cigarette in one hand and a half-full glass of Ricard in the other. I leaned on the doorjamb to watch, instantly aroused by the sway of her hips beneath the skin-tight scarlet satin of her stage dress. Sensing my presence, she half-turned her head and I could see that her lips were moving, miming to the English words of the song,

Some men like me talkin' happy
Some calls it snappy
Some call me honey
Others think I got money.

'Billie's Blues', I think it was called, by an American singer she had lately been obsessed with.

'It's lovely,' I said, 'but rather sad, I think.'

I was speaking to her profile, for a moment uncertain whether I was referring to the song or the woman who was miming the words of the singer, so breath-taking did I find her beauty.

When I was a boy my father, who had an interest in egyptology, encouraged me to accompany him on a week-long trip to Berlin and there, in the Neues Museum, he showed me the bust of Nefertiti, and I felt sure that she must have been the most beautiful lady who had ever lived. So when I first saw Ammarah singing on the street for a few sous, I could do nothing but stand and stare at the double of the woman figured in that bust – the swanlike arc of her neck, the almond eyes, high cheekbones, full lips and fine, straight nose; my personal archetype of womanly beauty.

She was, of course, much more than that, not all of it easy.

When I recall the events of that day, the day I met Ammarah, it is like following the action and the words of a script long written and re-written many times over, yet I know it could not have been like that.

To begin with, how did I persuade her to speak to me, to come with me? I hear myself saying, Come, and I see her come, but in life I must have invited her to join me for coffee at the café nearby. I can only imagine how tentatively the invitation must have been framed by that outworn version of myself, dazzled by her unattainable beauty and half-deafened by the blood-rush roar of my own desire and embarrassment.

And then she, being Ammarah, must have asked, why? And I would have stuttered and half-turned, about to withdraw, until she took pity on me. And later, when I admitted to being a policeman, I know that her nose must have wrinkled in disdain – I don't think I like policemen very much – yet I don't see it.

And what good reason she had to dislike policemen. Not just the ones who would harass her on the street and move her on, or demand 'favours' for letting her stay. No, not just those, because her father had been a policeman out in Senegal – one of those big white policemen who reign as satraps over dusty provincial realms of wandering fowl and goats. One of those policemen who has a cut in all the petty local action: the cognac evaporated from the barrel in the heat of the warehouse, the guns somehow lost in transit. One of those policemen whose word suffices to send a man to the guillotine, that first and finest avatar of the European enlightenment.

One of those policemen who has his pick of the women.

And Ammarah's father had picked her mother. And perhaps he had even come to love her after a fashion, because he brought her back to the motherland when his tour of duty came to an end. But this is not to say that he treated her at all kindly or well.

And, as for the daughter that she bore him? How did he look upon her as she grew into her beauty? He, who

36

was accustomed to power without limit, to possession without encumbrance? I don't know. Ammarah would not speak of it. But she left the sun-warmed terracotta of the south for the stone-cold streets of Paris for a reason.

'Well, don't just stand there, wind it up,' she said, a welcoming smile rising to her lips as she nodded towards the phonograph.

'Madame Maurer seemed concerned for you,' I said.

She deposited her glass on the polished lid of the grand piano, ash falling from her cigarette onto my parents' burnished parquet floor. I hurried forward with an ashtray and a coaster, provoking a pout and an amused lift of the perfect arch of her eyebrows.

'We should close the curtains,' I said, moving to do so. 'The blackout, you know...'

'What's the point? The Boches are probably here already, and they're bombing arms dumps and factories, not your bourgeois little apartment.'

She stubbed her cigarette out vehemently – in the ashtray, I was relieved to note. I ignored the contradiction and the provocation, and gently lowered the blackout blinds and drew the curtains closed.

'All the same... What's the matter? You're home very early.'

The song had finished. Ammarah wound the phonograph up for herself, angrily slapped a record onto the turntable – something by Louis Armstrong this time – and, flinging herself onto the sofa beside the drinks cabinet, poured herself another slug of Ricard.

I flinched at the careless sloshing of probably indelible liquid in such proximity to my mother's treasured Ruhlmann sofa, a somewhat impractical item of furniture in white and ebony, in a backless ottoman design.

I may have mentioned that my mother had an 'eye'. The salon was universally deemed proof of the fact, with its pair of Ruhlmann bergères, also white and ebony, its herd of elephant lamps, its veneered and lacquered drinks cabinet by Joubert, and its Leleu coffee table with three great feet like the clumping paws of some wooden ogre emerging from a central pillar beneath it and, prominent on its surface, a lamp by Lalique featuring the prancing form of some nymph or fertility goddess waving a bunch of grapes about.

The wallpaper behind the sofa depicted such a profusion of stylised tropical vegetation that, as a child, I had spent hours scrutinising it in dread of what fearsome beasts might lurk there.

'They've closed the club, just like that,' said Ammarah. 'Shut.'

I knew how great a blow this must be to her. With a regular spot, singing with the band at Ciao Ciao, she was beginning to make a name for herself, building a following, and the next step – a big step up – felt palpably close.

I could not allow her to sense the relief that rose in me at the thought that this step might now be postponed. In my jealous heart I feared her growing fame and the men it would draw to her – rich men, handsome men, powerful men. I saw that she was watching me closely, possibly sensing betrayal, and scrambled my way back to the moment.

'Who's closed the club? The authorities?'

I would expect to know if this was the case, but these were unusual times.

'Pino, the bastard. Just like that.' She was still glaring at me as though I were an accompanist playing in the wrong key.

Giuseppe 'Pino' Zagaria was the owner of the Ciao Ciao, a Neapolitan of shady reputation but, so far, no proven criminality.

I risked sitting next to her on the sofa, offering my shoulder to rest her head on. She did not push me away.

'Well,' I offered, 'lots of places are closing right now – hardly anything's open, in fact, but I expect things will start to come back when our new reality's established, whatever that will be. In hard times, people need music. Besides,' I added, remembering the news that had been running round the Quai des Orfèvres before I left, 'Italy's declared war on us, effective midnight, so I reckon Pino will find himself being led away by the plods in the morning.'

'Ha!' I could see that the news of Pino's likely incarceration had mollified her a little. 'But how am I supposed to feed myself in the meantime? Go back to singing on the streets?'

'Never. You can stay here with me – we won't go hungry.'

Now she did push me away, her dark eyes smouldering like coals, tears beginning to form.

'I told you from the start. I will never, ever be kept by any man.'

I said nothing, only opened my arms to her and waited for her to seek comfort in my mild embrace.

8

In the morning I woke to find the city smothered in impenetrable clouds of acrid black smoke.

I had intended to stroll along the Seine to the Quai de la Rapée for the autopsy of our unknown victim, but a few minutes in the choking air and the filthy black rain had me seeking refuge in the Métro at Hôtel de Ville. For once, the air was sweeter down there, though the heat was already building.

The ticket inspector to whom I showed my warrant card reckoned that the smoke was caused by officials burning papers at the ministries. On the platform, animated debates between the few remaining commuters ranged over any number of possibilities – our army laying down a smoke-screen to confuse the enemy, the Germans laying the smoke-screen to cover their entry into Paris, the Germans or perhaps the perfidious British bombing our oil depots. I even heard one old man declare that the smoke presaged the end of days. Later, Commissaire Roland told me that he had it from a stray army officer that our own high command had ordered the burning of oil reserves.

The black smoke had even infiltrated the roofed concourse of the Gare de Lyon, and I could taste it before I could see it, a sulphurous tarry substance precipitating from the air and coating the nasal passages and the tongue like some particularly foul medicine or, as our friend on the platform of Hôtel de Ville would have it, the fumes of hellfire.

The scene when I stepped up onto the concourse seemed, I had to concede, a pretty fair representation of the infernal abyss. Crowds were jostling and shouting, punches were thrown; children were crying and porters bellowing helplessly into the mob, trying to reunite them with their parents. A wailing toddler wearing wire-rimmed spectacles with one lens blacked out clung to the legs of a desperate railwayman, while an ageing policeman stood by, mopping his streaming brow with a large handkerchief, a distressed, helpless look in his eye.

'Thing is,' the railwayman was saying, 'Poor little bugger's so young he don't even know his name.'

No parents or guardians could be found to lay claim to the child.

A trestle table had been set up by the Red Cross and another by the Boy Scouts, offering directions, water and biscuits. But these heroic ventures in civic virtue were quite overwhelmed by the seething temper of the herd, and the ladies of the Red Cross huddled together for safety, ushering the younger boys into their midst lest they be trampled.

A trembling railway inspector told me that there were to be no more trains to the south. The announcement had just been made.

The mood felt so anarchic, so close to outright riot, that I did not care to flaunt my identity but simply threw myself into the steaming throng and heaved and thrust my way to the exit onto rue Bercy, where I found hordes still waiting in line to enter the station.

I pulled my hat down over my eyes for protection from the viscous black drizzle that continued to plop through the clouds of smoke from the sky and hastened towards the Institut médico-légal, where the autopsy was to take place.

The Institute, a long, deceptively low building, lurked behind a little park between the road and rail

41

bridges named for the battle of Austerlitz, quarantined from the human traffic of the city by a combination of roads, railways and water, as though it housed something contagious.

Across the road bridge, like an army of phantoms, a forlorn procession trudged through the dense clouds, heading south: old men and wounded veterans, women of all ages and classes, scared adolescents struggling to maintain the requisite pose of estrangement while clinging close to their mothers, younger children so silent and subdued that they might have been drugged, and babes in arms concerned only with milk and gentle arms to nestle in.

There were animals as well: dogs weaving between the legs and the wheels; a cow and a goat being led on halters, their ribs showing through their hides; chickens and ducks in wicker cages, canaries in wire ones, and one splendidly imperious scarlet macaw perched, as incongruous as a jewelled statuette, on the back of a rickety bicycle.

All manner of vehicles too: a pair of emaciated oxen straining to haul a cart which must have contained the family's every possession, a Renault piled high with the fruits of a life's labour, an obsolescent Citroën Type A which was giving off steam and surely destined to go no further; bicycles towing trolleys, innumerable handcarts and, for a family who could not muster so much as a handcart, an ancient pram; all heaped with as much as could be loaded onto them and topped, in nearly every case, by a mattress.

I realised, with a spasm of grief for my country, that these people in flight from an invading army – from all points north and east of Paris, and from Belgium too – had little expectation of ever returning to their homes. You do not take your mattress with you when you believe you will be coming home.

I turned away from this dismal retreat and walked through the garden square towards the Institute. Exhausted refugees squatted and sprawled everywhere, finding a few minutes respite from the relentless march, and a small group of unarmed and bedraggled soldiers surrounded the single bench, taking turns to swig from a bottle. Dead-eyed and swaying, they resembled nothing so much as a bunch of demoralised scarecrows.

Drink and despair had loosened their lips and, as I passed, I heard one of them declare, 'Shit on your war!'

Another smashed the empty bottle to the ground and took up the theme, loudly declaiming into the enveloping darkness, 'Fuck the Republic! Fuck France!'

I averted my eyes and hurried past, desperate to avoid attracting their attention.

9

Within the Institute all was at peace and in order, as befitted a place dedicated to the dead. Commissaire Roland was waiting for me at the door to the mortuary. We had barely greeted each other when the door opened and the cropped square head of the mortuary porter, Hubert, popped out.

'His nibs says you're three minutes late but you'd better come in,' he announced with his habitual sourness.

In all the years of our professional acquaintance, I never did discover whether Hubert was the cantankerous fellow's first or second name.

'His nibs' was Professor Marcel de Chevigny, the first holder of the chair of morbid anatomy and forensic science in the school of surgery at the Sorbonne and the Salpêtrière, and the director of the Institut médico-légal of Paris.

The corpse lay in front of him, uncovered on the mortuary table. A tall man, well-built, Hubert's neat needlework already evident, refastening the cadaver along the Y of the professor's customary incision from shoulders to pubis, like one of those zip fasteners.

I fixed my eyes on the torso, resolving that I would inspect the more troubling aspects of our victim's person only when called upon to do so.

'I see you've already been busy, Prof,' said Roland.

'What else is there to do in these dark times but work?' de Chevigny replied. 'Sleep is out of the question.'

His voice was gentle and courteous. I did not for a moment believe Hubert's suggestion that he had expressed impatience with our supposed unpunctuality.

'Is it?' asked Roland in the baffled tone of one who had never in his life lost sleep through worry. 'This is a surprise,' he said, pointing with his pencil at the man's genitals which, like the face and the skin of the thigh, had been devastated by the corrosive liquid.

This, of course, was the same mutilation from which I had been trying to avert my eyes, all the while finding my horrified gaze drawn inexorably towards it.

'The effect of concentrated sulphuric acid, thrown into the face and pooling in the poor man's lap – post-mortem, I am relieved to say.'

'Sulphuric acid, you say,' Roland noted it. 'Who might have access to that?'

'I'm afraid it's used quite widely – domestically in clearing drains, industrially in the manufacture of fertiliser, in the production of steel... printing, paper-making, chemical laboratories... It wouldn't be at all difficult to obtain.'

He stroked his silver goatee beard regretfully as he delivered this unhelpful information. The dome of his bald head shone under the bright lights of the autopsy room, his fine, rather feminine features inclined towards the commissaire.

Roland nodded as though he had thought this would be the case.

'Well, Prof, what can you tell us?'

'The victim was a healthy male of about thirty, though from the fatty changes in his liver he probably drank to some excess. What is it I always say, Inspector?'

'Never more than a litre a day,' I intoned dutifully.

'Quite. There was no evidence of active disease, no recent injury, no notable distinguishing features –

45

Hubert has taken his fingerprints for you. Only the fatal wound and the rather puzzling treatment of the body post-mortem. And I can't be certain, given the effects of the acid, but I think he was probably circumcised.'

'An israélite then,' I suggested, not adding, 'like me.'

'Not necessarily,' said Roland, looking at me as though to say it's not always about you. 'Could be an arab or an american...'

'Or the procedure is sometimes carried out, usually in childhood, to treat phimosis,' the professor offered, 'a tightness of the foreskin so that it cannot be retracted, sometimes leading to extremely painful infections.'

'What about the fatal wound?' Roland asked.

'Could you bring the brain please, Hubert,' the professor said by way of reply, 'and then turn the body so that we might examine the entry wound.'

The technician lumbered over with a covered kidney dish held before him like a sacrificial offering, grumbling under his breath.

'Thank you so much, old friend,' said de Chevigny without a trace of irritation or condescension. 'Now, the blade – it is, as you suggested, Arthur, likely to have been an ice-pick – entered here in the midline between the first and second vertebrae, known as the atlas and the axis, and was thrust upwards and forwards with considerable force, penetrating the medulla oblongata here,' he demonstrated the spot on one of the slices of offal in the kidney dish with an anatomist's pointer, 'and passing through the posterior compartment of the foramen magnum into the brainstem, here, causing catastrophic injury, the cessation of vital functions and instant death.

'The immediate withdrawal of the blade acted, if you will, as a kind of superfluous coup de grâce by provoking a devastating haemorrhage into the space created and the adjoining brain tissue, utterly destroying the pons.

46

He was likely to have been looking down, the neck flexed, thus,' he reached up to grasp Roland's head and produce the correct angle, 'causing the gap between the posterior arch of the atlas and the lamina of the axis to widen to its maximum, here.'

He tapped a spot on the back of Roland's neck. I wondered what our victim had been looking at – no reading material had been found at the scene – or whether he had perhaps been fortunate enough to be dozing.

'In other words, he was pithed like a laboratory frog,' said Roland.

'Precisely so. This was, as you surmised, the work of an expert – the point of entry, the angle of the blade, the degree of force and, finally, the withdrawal, the haemorrhage. Premeditated and unsurvivable.'

'All exactly as Dr Caron described it with hardly more than a glance at the wound,' Roland muttered to me. 'That young man knows what he's talking about – one way or another.'

10

A call from Nevin was put through to the post-mortem room just as we were finishing with Professor de Chevigny. Hubert passed the receiver to Roland with all the good grace of a dog obliged to surrender its dinner, and the commissaire listened and took notes, thanked Nevin, praised him for his diligence and beckoned me over.

'That batch of first-class tickets was divided between these five tabacs near Reuilly-Diderot Métro station.' He handed me the page from his notebook. 'Cut over there and see if you can find out who bought a carnet of them. I've got something on, so I'll see you back at '36' at about twelve – we'll go for lunch and take stock then.'

I couldn't face Gare de Lyon again, so I walked by back streets through the oily smog, avoiding the doleful caravan of refugees along Boulevard Diderot. After fifteen minutes, my chosen route brought me to rue Érard, where one of the café-tabacs on the list was situated.

It hadn't much felt like it so far, but it was about to turn into my lucky day. Even the choking smog was beginning to melt away.

The narrow frontage of Les Garçons Noirs was secreted between the plate windows and bright signage of a butcher's shop and the rococo gilt of a patisserie, though both of these were closed on Tuesday in compliance with the recent edict. Unless, I reflected, the proprietors and their families had fled the city and shut their businesses indefinitely.

Only the red Tabac sign drew the eye to the café which, at a first glance, also appeared to be closed, so little light or evidence of life escaped its self-effacing windows. No tables or chairs on the pavement enticed passers-by to sit for a rest and warm croissants and coffee, and the gilt lettering on the window – LIQ U S D ARQ – was as baffling as a newspaper puzzle. I pushed at the door, which bore a number of peeling stickers – 'Byrrh', 'Johnnie Walker', 'Bass Pale Ale' – and entered.

Though narrow, the room was surprisingly deep. The guéridons and chairs which should have been outside were still stacked between the entrance and the counter. In the far corner the only customers were a shabby, elderly couple who nursed what looked like glasses of cheap brandy, smoke from their cigarettes swirling up towards an inert ceiling-fan. They appeared to be arguing.

From behind the zinc counter a blonde woman in early middle-age regarded me stonily. The grey at her roots suggested she had all but given up, but not quite – her apron was gleaming white and so stiff with starch that she crackled when she moved. On a shelf above the depleted racks of cigarettes and spirits behind her, a wireless set muttered despairingly to itself about the state of the war. I was grateful to notice a pot of coffee gently steaming on the hob at her side.

Since the patisserie was closed, there was no basket of croissants and rolls to tempt patrons to take breakfast, but there was a desultory array of stale madeleines on a plate. I ordered a coffee, took a stool at the bar, and smiled at the woman as she poured from the pot. A large fly settled on a madeleine.

'Grim out there in that fog this morning. Any news on what's caused it?' I said, nodding in the direction of the radio.

'I don't listen any more,' she said. 'Want a madeleine with that?'

Anticipating a refusal, she turned away and began to wipe the shelves behind her.

49

'Yes please,' I said to regain her attention, keeping a bilious eye on the fly. 'I think I will.'

She grimaced as if to say, 'Really?'

Behind me the volume was rising in the row between the early drinkers. As she handed me the madeleine on a napkin, I placed my PJ warrant card on the counter.

'It must be hard for you, here on your own.'

Her eyes flicked to my ID and back to some place behind my left shoulder. I pocketed it.

'I have the boy to help... when he cares to.' I guessed she was referring to her son.

Over in the far corner, a chair clattered to the floor and the woman shrieked, 'You piece of shit!'

I turned and watched as she bustled furiously past us, one hand holding her little hat steady on her head, and slammed the door behind her as she left. The old man's head had slumped onto the table – perhaps he had fallen asleep.

'She'll be back,' said the café owner, smiling for the first time.

I took my opportunity.

'I wonder if you could help me,' I said, hastily adding, 'Don't worry, it's not about your son.'

She sighed, and I thought I could see tears forming in her eyes.

'Why not have a coffee and a sit down with me,' I suggested. 'It's not as if you're run off your feet...'

Mutely, she poured herself a coffee and came to join me at a table near the window. I left the madeleine on the counter.

'All I need to know is if anyone bought a carnet of first-class tickets here in the last few days,' I said.

She smiled again, out of relief, I thought, catching a sudden glimpse of the bright and hopeful young woman who had once inhabited these careworn features.

'There's only one person ever bought a first-class ticket in here,' she said, glancing at the patch of linoleum in front of the door, where the canvas backing was showing. 'But, still, they make us carry a stock.'

'Really? Who is that?'

'They call him Tommy or Tom Pouce, on account of him being such a big man – it's a joke between them, see?'

She required no prompting to describe 'Tommy', whom she had clearly taken to – a tall man, very handsome with thick dark brown hair, 'beautiful' brown eyes and a strong nose. He was a snappy dresser, her Tommy, and never short of money – always left a generous tip. He was beginning to sound very much like our man.

'When did he last buy Métro tickets here?'

'Why, yesterday afternoon – he came in just for the tickets, just him, on his own.'

'What was he wearing?'

'Blue suit, that lovely brown hat,' she replied dreamily. I would still have to check the other cafés, but I was certain this was him.

'Do you know his full name?' She shook her head, pursing her lips as though she was trying to remember if she had ever heard it. 'You said they call him... Who are they?'

'He's often in here with a bunch of old legionnaires – not all of them gentlemen, not like Tommy. They sit at the back, play cards, drink, talk about what men talk about...'

I raised an interrogative eyebrow.

'You know, women, the old days in the Legion, politics, work...'

'Had Tommy been in the Foreign Legion then? He was foreign?'

'You'd hardly have known it, his French is that good – educated, you know? But, yes, I'm pretty sure he'd been in the Legion.'

'He drank a lot, Tommy?'

'They all do. Not that I ever saw him drunk – like I said, he's a gentleman.'

'And this work they talked about?'

She hesitated, and I sensed that she was calculating the likelihood that she was talking Tommy into trouble. A customer entered and, grunting and sighing with the aches and pains of a woman's lot, manoeuvred herself into position at a nearby table like a ship coming into her home port after too long an absence.

'Oh, Katrine, chérie,' she appealed to the proprietress, 'can't we have some music on the wireless, instead of this crap?'

'Good morning to you too,' said Katrine, rising to attend to the woman, but she was smiling. 'Your usual?'

After changing the station on the radio and bringing the woman a pastis, a black coffee and a carafe of water, she returned to my table with another coffee for me.

'On the house,' she said. 'And you forgot this,' producing the final item from the tin tray that she was expertly bearing on one hand – my madeleine.

'Sit down, Katrine,' I said. 'And don't worry, Tommy is not in any trouble with us. What work?'

11

The restaurant was a little establishment in Place Dauphine, just around the corner from 36. Roland had already ordered for both of us – a green salad followed by baked river trout with a dill sauce and parmentier potatoes.

'I felt such a fool,' I said, taking my seat across the table from him. 'I was so pleased with identifying our man in the first café on the list that I wanted to phone you straight away. I even asked the woman for a jeton.'

'You forgot public phones have been cut off? It'll take some getting used to – it's force of habit, isn't it?'

He settled back in his chair, tucking the white table napkin into his shirt at the neck in the manner of a peasant farmer at a daughter's wedding feast.

'You checked the other tabacs?'

'Of course. None of them had sold a first-class ticket in weeks. It's just not a first-class part of the world, I suppose. Anyway, this is our man, no doubt about it – right description, right clothes on the day, right tickets. I checked the numbers on the ones she had left.'

'Got a name, this bloke?'

By some act of prestidigitation, his green salad and most of the bread basket had disappeared before I'd picked up my fork.

'Tommy, or Tom Pouce – a nickname because he was tall. He was a veteran of the Foreign Legion. A gentleman, she said, but a drinker all right.'

'Surname?'

'She doesn't know. But she reckons he and his ex-Legion pals have got the door security racket all sewn up in the clubs and bals-musettes around the Bastille – rue de Lappe, Passage Thiéré, those places. Probably did a bit of pimping and dope-dealing on the side – from her account he had plenty of cash.'

'Any idea which clubs and dancehalls?'

The fish had arrived, and the waiter was at our elbows taking it cleanly off the bone with the slick efficiency of a Métro dipper lifting a drunk man's wallet. I waited while he dressed the trout and put the plates and the dish of potatoes in front of us.

'Not really,' I said as the waiter left us to it. 'I'll have to go over there this afternoon and see what's what.'

'Not on your own, you won't. I'd get nothing back but your bones and teeth.'

I noticed that he made no reference to my hair, and found myself staring mournfully into my reflection in the mirror behind him. My hair was not so much receding as residual, literally marginal.

'We'll go together,' he decreed.

As we sipped our coffees – still the real stuff then – Roland leaned in to speak urgently and confidentially.

'Simon, you should think about getting out. This war's lost, Paris will fall within days, and the Germans will be in full control. Maybe their army works by some sort of normal military code but what will ride in on its coat-tails doesn't. Believe me – I've seen it in action, and it's lawless, vicious and completely insane.'

'You mean they don't like Jews.'

'It's worse than you can know. Look, you remember that I went to Berlin on a case in '38, don't you? Well, in all the time I was there, the Gestapo followed me every step of the way and they made sure I knew they were there. They wanted me to fear them, right? But they couldn't stop me seeing what was there in plain sight, shameless. These people hate Jews, Jojo, they smash up their homes and businesses and throw them on the street, they beat them, arrest them, kill them sometimes. It's policy, Jojo. Violent crime is the policy of that rotten

54

state and it's going to get worse. The violent criminal always steps up, not down, until he's stopped. You know that.

'I was invited to have dinner with Heydrich, the head of the Gestapo, did you know that? Couldn't get out of it. Almost put me off my food.'

He smiled but his gaze was unrelenting, intense.

'He's a smooth operator, all right: intelligent, handsome – the son of an opera singer, he told me – all polite talk and knowing his wine and dabbing at the corner of his mouth with a serviette, but he was cold. I don't think I've ever before looked a man in the eye and shivered. But I sat there and I shivered, I tell you. It was like looking into the eyes of a crocodile – inhuman, merciless, deadly. You know I've sat across the table from some right disgusting specimens in my time, but none like him, I swear it. He freezes the air in the room, that man.

'And then, when it was time to leave the restaurant, the other customers – all but one or two – they insisted on escorting him, us, to his car, bowing and scraping and arms up in the air, saluting and shouting "Heil Hitler", as though it was some kind of religion and he the high priest or some such. I've never seen anything so sickening. And he stood there, cool as you like, half a smile on those thin lips, and he did something, some tiny gesture of command – I didn't even see what it was – and they scuttled back to their tables, eyes down.

'Do you hear what I'm saying, Jojo? Do you see it? They've bought it, the German people – or most of them have – and they'll believe anything and do anything these wretches tell them. It's a madhouse, it's going to be a slaughter-house, and it's coming here. You're not safe. Leave while you can.'

'I'm going nowhere, boss. I had to fight hard and risk everything to be a detective, and I'm not giving it up now, I'm not running.'

Roland sat back and regarded me in silence while he picked at his teeth with a thumbnail. He knew about the antisemitism that made it all but impossible for an israélite to make his way in the PJ, and probably thought that was what I was talking about, but he couldn't possibly understand the intensity of the opposition my family had brought to the matter, the rows, the tears.

'All right,' he said finally. 'We'll have to find another way.'

So abnormal, so dreamlike, was the atmosphere in Paris in those last days before the fall that the proprietor quite forgot to protest when Roland insisted on paying our bill, but he did bustle to the door ahead of us and see us out with a bow and his best smile. In the dusty square, the oily fog and drizzle had cleared completely, and we walked out into a perfect summer afternoon.

'Tell me,' said Roland as we crossed the river in bright sunlight to catch the Métro at Châtelet, 'What did your parents want you to be, if not a detective?'

I looked at him sharply and nearly laughed aloud at this new evidence of his strange, untutored omniscience.

'My father thought I might become an archaeologist.'

'Same thing,' he said, looking straight ahead. 'Digging.'

12

Surprisingly few of the bals musettes and clubs in rue de Lappe had defied January's edict closing them for the duration, and those that were not barred and shuttered would not open to the public until the evening. One or two showed signs of life, however, and these would do for a start.

'Tom Pouce' turned out to be a rather well-known person in these parts, but no one would admit to knowing him well. It was only when I spotted Pino Zagaria, the owner-manager of the Ciao Ciao, sitting on the step of his club in his undervest, disconsolately smoking, that we began to get somewhere.

'Hello, Pino,' I said. 'They've not yet picked you up then?'

Roland waited across the road, pretending to survey the scant goods left in an Auvergnat épicerie – a ring of dried sausage, a fly-blown ham, a few jars of confit duck. For such a big man he was remarkably adept at making himself inconspicuous.

'They came, Inspector, they came all right,' he said, 'but I was "out" if you know what I mean.'

'Well, your secret's safe with me – doesn't make sense, does it, interning innocent men like you?' Innocent was, to say the least, an inexact description of Giuseppe Zagaria, but needs must...

'Fucking Mussolini! That fat fuck of a poncing, posing cunt.'

He ground the butt of his cigarette under a built-up heel with unnecessary force, hawked and spat venomously. A well-formed gob of phlegm described a long arc in the soft summer air and landed in the cobbled carriageway.

57

'Ammarah's very upset at losing her spot, you know.'

He sighed and shrugged hugely to demonstrate his immense impotence in the matter.

'What can a man do? I couldn't keep the club open, turn up every night and wait for them to come and arrest me, and I'm not going to let anyone else run my club and fuck me up the arse and run off with the takings, am I?'

'Why do you imagine anyone would do that to you?'

'I would,' he replied in a pragmatic tone of voice. 'It's business, isn't it?'

I lit a cigarette for him, and one for me.

'I'll do what I can to help, but I wonder if you could help me too?'

He could. Pino knew 'Tom Thumb' – he used the English name, pronounced with Neapolitan panache – and, more importantly, he knew where he worked most often. I beckoned the commissaire across. Pino eyed him with distaste and spat in the dust at his feet.

'I know who he is,' he said when I tried to effect an introduction. 'You want La Salle En Haut in Passage Thiéré, hotel below, dancefloor above – makes no sense. Just don't tell them Pino sent you.'

The hotel was called Les Quatre Saisons, but there was nothing of spring or summer about it. It presented a façade of smoke-grimed peeling stucco behind which, I suspected, lay a squalor of décor and drains that would harmonise perfectly with the character of its residents, whether semi-permanent or barely transient.

I had seen many such establishments before – rooms by the day or the hour – and they were always the same, harbouring a collective of petty criminals, good time girls on the way down, travelling salesmen and con artists, and poor old devils who had been abandoned by time and their families, and had nowhere else to be.

A sign suspended over an iron staircase running up the side of the building announced La Salle En Haut, Bal-Musette in letters picked out by coloured lightbulbs, alongside crude representations of an accordion and a few random musical notes. The door at the top of the stairs was open, allowing the stinks of the night before – sweat, cigarette smoke, something fishy – to escape into the city.

We stood just inside the door, allowing our eyes to become accustomed to the gloom. Only the cleaner – an elegant African woman, her cheeks bearing the marks of scarification – moved about the place, skating over the dance floor with a mop as though an invisible band played in her head. At the far end of the dance floor, beside the sign pointing to the WC, was the dais on which the real musicians would perform each night. It looked about the size of my parents' piano.

Roland removed his hat and addressed the cleaning woman without raising his voice, bringing her to an immediate halt: 'The manager in, madame?'

She glanced towards a closed door behind the bar.

'Thank you, madame,' said Roland, indicating with a flick of the head that I should come with him.

The door gave onto a narrow, unlit corridor with one door to our left and another straight ahead. I guessed the one on the left opened into the cloakroom, whose hatch was just inside the entrance of the place.

Roland stepped forward and flung the other door open, revealing a small man with black, greased-back hair seated behind a desk the size of a tennis court. He wore a white tuxedo and a valentino moustache, and in his right hand he held a revolver aimed straight at Roland's heart.

13

'Not a good idea, Claude,' said Roland, reaching across the desk to snatch the piece from an unresisting hand.

I recognised him now – Claude 'Crapaud' Rospeau, a versatile career criminal who had served sentences for armed robbery, fraud, blackmail and sundry other offences since his teens.

Roland emptied the magazine and pocketed the pistol.

'Hey,' whined Rospeau, 'that's mine.'

'Legally?' Roland directed an arched eyebrow at him. 'Anyway, who's got you messing your pants? Who did you expect to be walking through that door?'

Rospeau grimaced but said nothing for several seconds. I could see his cunning little mind working, seeking a plausible answer like a dog quartering a field in search of a lost ball.

'The Boches,' he said finally. 'People say they're already here.'

'Pull the other one,' said Roland with a fleeting, wintery smile at the thought of 'Crapaud' the patriotic hero.

'When the Germans come,' I added, leaning over the desk so that he could feel my breath in his face, 'your tongue will be so far up their arses you'll taste the sauerkraut.'

Rospeau shrugged and went over my head to the commissaire.

'Look, Monsieur Roland, you know me, I'll do what I can to help if you'd just tell me...'

'Why do you think we're here, Claude?'

Roland often played the game of interrogation as though it were a particularly attritional game of rugby football – give nothing, make ground metre by hard metre.

Rospeau shrugged again. He wasn't going to say anything that disclosed the nature of whatever underworld grievance or vendetta currently engrossed and terrified him.

'I don't know,' he said, 'how could I? I'm straight now, you know that, Monsieur Roland.'

'Do I?' Roland was picking his teeth with a matchstick taken from a book on the desk.

Rospeau was wide-eyed with indignation that Roland should cast the slightest shadow on his sunlit innocence.

Roland sighed, 'It's just clearing something up, Claude – a boring bit of administration about Tommy... Tom Pouce, the door guy.'

Rospeau almost fainted with relief.

'Anything, Monsieur Commissaire. How can I help? Is it a licensing thing, something like that?'

Roland took out his notebook, licked his pencil in the downbeat, dull-eyed manner of one who is about to embark on a bureaucratic task of the most soporific tedium.

'Could you describe the gentleman in as much detail as possible?'

Rospeau's description fitted our victim and the man described by the café-owner, nailing the identification.

'And could you confirm his full name and address?' said Roland in the same disinterested monotone.

Rospeau nodded and swung round in his chair to reach for a ledger on the shelf behind him. The backs of his hands were covered with warty excrescences. His fingers brushed the much-repaired cover of the book and recoiled as though burnt.

'What is this?' he said, swinging back round to look up at the commissaire. 'You don't even know his name?'

'Get the book, Claude.' Roland's voice had acquired a hard, authoritative edge.

Rospeau planted his feet firmly under the desk and settled more deeply into his chair, sneering up at us.

'You get nothing without a warrant, commissaire, can't do it. Sorry, but that's the law.'

He folded his warty hands on his developing belly and sighed with self-righteous satisfaction.

Roland reached across and, hauling him to his feet with one mighty hand grasping both lapels, brought his head down so that their noses were almost touching.

'Well, I'm glad to be able to help you out of your little legal difficulty, Claude,' he said with a leonine smile, his big yellow teeth showing. 'I've got a commission rogatoire in my pocket, signed by Judge Leclerc. Would you like to see it?'

Rospeau raised his hands as if in surrender.

'No need for that, monsieur commissaire – I take your word, of course. Just... have to be all above board and legal, don't we?'

Roland released him and he collapsed back into the chair and wheeled around to grab the ledger and drop it onto the desk with a thump. Hastily, mopping sweat from his brow as he went, he leafed through the pages until he found what he was after.

'So fucking hot in here,' he muttered as he turned the book around so that we could read it. 'See here, the name I've got for him is Thomas Fabricant, but of course that won't be his real name, him having been in the Legion and that – he'll have had some bloody foreign name, won't he? And the address I've got is in rue Mesnil in the sixteenth, see, there.'

He tapped on the page with a warty finger. In a belated epiphany I realised why they called him 'the Toad'.

'Swanky,' I said with an involuntary sidelong glance at Roland, whose address was even more incongruously exclusive.

'Yeah, well,' said Rospeau, relaxed and in a confiding mood now he considered that the pressure was off, 'our Tommy has some powerful friends, doesn't he. And with powerful friends,' he looked at us slyly, 'you make some powerful enemies too, no? Is that what this is about?'

Roland ignored the question.

'What kind of friends?'

'Politics – I keep out of that kind of shit, myself.' He turned to appeal to me, 'What did politics ever do for us – people like you and me, inspector, honest suckers out to scrape a living? I said to Tommy, I said, you want to be more careful about the people you mix with, or you'll find yourself in trouble, I said. Is he? Is he in trouble? I told him...'

His expression was serious, sincere, betraying no hint of irony.

'What kind of politics?' Roland demanded, ignoring Rospeau's question.

'What kinds are there? I don't know... the patriots, you know, the ones who stand up to the commies and the yids...'

I felt the familiar shock run through me, as though I had inadvertently touched the live wire – again.

Roland ploughed on, his gaze and voice stern and level.

'Which group? The CDFC?'

Rospeau shrugged. He knew he'd said too much, but he couldn't take it back now. He'd never heard of the acronym on the badge worn by our corpse though. I'd have sworn to that.

'Which group?' Roland repeated, 'Action Française, the Croix de Feu, the PPF, the Cagoule?'

Rospeau stiffened, almost imperceptibly, his gaze suddenly eluding that of Roland, only to find my face hardening in contemptuous fury.

Roland spelled it out for him, 'The Comité secret d'action révolutionnaire, eh? Or what's left of it.'

The extreme-rightist Cagoule had seen a wave of arrests and prosecutions following its bomb outrages in Paris a couple of years earlier.

'And what, exactly, did "Tommy" have to do with that bunch of ponces, thugs and maniacs? Names, Claude, names – now.'

Rospeau jumped to his feet, pale and sweating profusely, as though he, in turn, had been electrified.

'Nothing more to say,' he muttered, taking out a handkerchief from his top pocket.

'We'll decide when you've nothing more to say,' I interjected, hitting the desk with the flat of my hand. 'Give us names, unless you want us to run you in for the unlicensed knocking shop you're running downstairs; not to mention keeping this flea-bitten dance hall open in defiance of the law.'

He flinched and I knew I had guessed right about the hotel.

'No, no,' he whined, 'we're not open for dancing no more, just a bar, you know... And downstairs, it's not... it's just... if a couple's getting too fresh on the dance floor, we let them... It's a service.'

'Or perhaps you'd like us to turn this place upside down and inside out in a thorough search?' I suggested.

'Search? Search for what?'

'Oh, I'm sure we'd find something,' Roland said pleasantly.

Rospeau flopped back into his seat, mopping his face like a sailor swabbing the quarterdeck.

'He had a girl here – Louise. She still works the bar. Come back at seven and you'll find her setting up. She knows him better than I do.'

We were putting on our hats to leave when Roland startled Rospeau with a final question.

'Place like this,' he said casually, 'I'm surprised you bother with names and addresses of doormen. Why?'

When Rospeau laughed, he reminded me of a shark.

'Tommy banks the takings for me, sometimes. A man has his hands on my money, I want to know where to find him.'

14

'If he knows Tommy is dead, he's a hell of an actor,' I said to Roland once we had gained the street, where the unmarked car ordered by Roland was waiting for us.

'He isn't. He doesn't. Rue Mesnil,' he said to the driver. 'Better move it, in case that fellow phones ahead of us.'

I would have deployed a saltier epithet when speaking of a lowlife creep like Rospeau, but I never heard Roland swear – well, just the once, and we'll come to that in due course.

Rue Mesnil was a quiet, nondescript street running from Saint-Honoré d'Eylau church on Place Victor-Hugo down to rue Saint-Didier. Smart apartment blocks, shops (mostly closed and shuttered) and cafés; a covered market, a couple of restaurants and, plonked down among it all like a carelessly planted boot, a brand new fire station complete with barracks and married quarters above.

At the address we'd been given by Rospeau the ground floor windows were barred and the heavy street door was locked. Beside it was a single bell push, presumably connected to the concierge's quarters, and a steel postbox securely bolted to the wall. Nothing proclaimed the identity of any occupant of the building. Roland took all of this in and immediately made for the café across the road.

'Time for a coffee, I think,' he said, quietly adding, 'Don't look back. What does this place remind you of?'

'Um, a prison? An asylum? A barracks?'

'Before opening the café door he said, 'Did you spot the lookout, second floor? That's a fortress, that is.'

Behind the zinc counter of the café a stout man was leaning on his elbows, puffing diligently on a long-stemmed Vuillard pipe.

'Gents?' he inquired disinterestedly.

Roland ordered two coffees and we stood at the bar as we sipped them and attempted gently to mine the man for information. What was that place opposite, we asked. He shrugged. Do they come in here much, we wondered. He shrugged again.

'Lots of people do.'

Strange sort of place, isn't it, we mused, all locked up like that.

'Not my business,' he said, implying it was none of ours either.

'Only we think a friend of ours might live there,' I said. 'Name of Tommy. Some people call him Tom Pouce, on account of his being quite a big sort of fellow.'

He could not help glancing at the hulk that was Roland.

'Don't know him,' he said, and began to refill his pipe from a jar beneath the counter.

'I do know you from somewhere though,' he said to Roland, his eyes narrowing. 'Where's that now?'

I noticed for the first time that he had a sizeable dent on the right side of his head – another wounded veteran of the last war.

'Could be anywhere,' said Roland, quietly laying his warrant card on the counter. 'I tend to stand out from the crowd.'

'No, that's not it,' the man said, looking at the warrant card. 'But I know that name, all right – I saw your last game for France.'

In the presence of a sporting hero the man had quite forgotten to persist in his surliness. He smiled and leaned across the counter to pat Roland fondly on the arm.

67

'Le Bourreau himself,' he said, 'in my café...'

Behind him the door to the dark hinterland of the café opened and a tousled head popped out.

'For Christ's sake, Simon,' said the head, 'you and your boss need to bugger off fast, before anyone sees you.'

I recognised Gaspard Raban, who had moved onto the Central Intelligence Bureau after we had briefly served together in the Marais.

'I have a murder to investigate,' Roland said, 'so I'm not moving. You'd better take us to your boss, Raban, and we'll see what's what.'

15

Commissaire Xavier Six of the Central Intelligence Bureau – known to all but himself as 'Double-X', since he bore the uncommon distinction of a name beginning and ending with the symbol denoting an unknown quantity – was waiting for us upstairs.

Lean and of middling height, he wore a little black beard like that of a music hall magician, and his bright black eyes glanced and glinted like those of a magpie sizing up a corpse. I had never encountered anyone who looked more conspicuously like a spy.

From the slight elevation of one black eyebrow and the tapping of a dainty patent leather shoe on the floor I understood that he was furious.

'Afternoon, Xavier,' said Roland. 'Fancy meeting you here.'

He cast a sceptical glance over the assemblage of surveillance equipment in the little bedroom, apparently impervious to the derisive expressions on the faces of Six's men.

'What are you doing here, Roland, trampling all over my investigation?'

The voice was curiously reedy and somehow polyphonic, as though he spoke through a harmonica.

'Looking for a murderer, Xavier. At the moment we're trying to understand who the victim was and what he might have been up to. How about you?'

Despite himself, Six was interested – call it the detective's compulsive curiosity – 'What have you got?'

Roland produced our photographs of the victim at the crime scene from an inside pocket and laid them where he could find space on the narrow bed.

'Seems to be a chap who goes by the name of Thomas Fabricant – ex-FL, works the door at clubs and the like around Bastille, might have some connections in dodgy politics. People call him "Tommy" or "Tom Pouce".'

A quick, involuntary glance was exchanged between Six and Raban. I saw that Roland had not missed it.

'The only address we have for him is the place over there that you seem to be watching. Know him?'

Raban winced as they inspected the photos, in which the obliteration of the man's face was captured in sharp focus. Six tapped one of the photos - the one that showed our man seated, head bowed in the attitude of a commuter dozing on a train – and glared up at Roland with the ferocity of a viper about to bite.

'I should have been informed,' he said. 'You should have consulted me before you came clumping around here.'

'I would have, if I'd known you were watching the place, but you lot are so secretive...'

'With half the police force either touting for hire or already owned by these bastards, you're damned right we're secretive.'

Roland looked at him so mournfully that Six laughed.

'All right, all right, I know you're clean, Arthur.'

He inspected the photograph again, holding it up to the light near the window, stroking his little beard as though deep in thought.

'How was your man killed?'

'Professionally, I'd say – ice-pick to the base of the skull, straight into the brain, instant death where he sat on the Métro – in the first-class carriage. The killer just vanished, possibly at Saint-Paul – one man was seen running from the station, and we're looking for him – but our man could have got off earlier... lost himself in the crowds at Gare de Lyon perhaps. Not much to go on.'

70

'No, not much.' Six frowned and lowered his head, pinching his nose as though to suppress a sneeze. 'Look, Arthur, I'll give you this much. Thomas Fabricant is... was an associate of our friends over the road, and he did sometimes stay there. He and some of his old pals from the Legion provided a bit of threat, a bit of muscle when it was needed; maybe, in your man's case, something more – unlike most of them he had a brain as well as brawn – but I wouldn't know anything about that.'

'He seems to have had plenty of money – look at his clothes. Where from? Who are these people?'

Six appeared to give this question a great deal of thought before he responded.

'Good question. We thought we'd finished the Cagoule in '38, but maybe we'd just smashed the mirror – into lots of little mirrors. This looks like some kind of revivalist group – some of the old faces have reappeared in Paris and we need to know what they're up to – but things aren't altogether well between them. It looks as though there's a split over how to react when the Germans come. Patriotism or power, if you catch my drift.'

Roland nodded, thunderclouds gathering on his face. 'So Fabricant could have been caught up in some kind of internal warfare – killed by one side or the other?'

Six nodded ruminatively. 'Perhaps, but I can't let you poke around in that ants' nest over there, not now. The rumour I'm hearing – and I'm sure you are too – is that Paris will be declared an open city, left undefended in order to save it from destruction.'

I felt sure that this was no rumour – that Six had been told this by the prefect, Langeron, who would have had it directly from Mandel, the minister of the interior.

'Arthur, I need to see this thing through, get a clear understanding of where all these cards are falling before the enemy walks in. This could be a matter of life or death for a sovereign, republican France – perhaps even more so than the damned war itself.'

'One last thing and we'll be out of your hair. Recognise this?' Roland produced the little gold badge that the victim had worn at the back of his lapel.

Six turned it over and over in his hand. Again he and Raban exchanged glances.

'CDFC,' he said, 'Chevaliers de la France Catholique. It's the name some of them like to go under these days. New name, same shit.'

16

They allowed Roland to use their telephone to call 36. He spoke briefly to Nevin, giving him the task of tracing Thomas Fabricant's Foreign Legion records and, if possible, establishing our victim's origin and true identity.

Our car was waiting for us where we'd left it in Place Victor-Hugo, the driver leaning against the bonnet, smoking and chatting to a couple of young girls. It looked almost like a normal summer scene. Only the continual rumble of distant gunfire punctured the illusion.

'Back to Passage Thiéré,' said Roland, sliding across the back seat before the driver had had the chance to stub out his Caporal.

We proceeded by back roads, avoiding as far as possible the bridges and the main routes from the north and east, along which the flood of the frightened and the dispossessed continued without cease. Even so, it took half an hour to get as far as the unavoidable thoroughfare of Boulevard de Sebastopol, and there we came to a definitive halt.

At the junction with Rue Étienne-Marcel a crowd had gathered to witness the pitiable spectacle of a black mare, collapsed and obviously dying between the shafts of an overloaded cart.

The distraught farmer, caught between rage and despair, shouted to the heavens and swore vengeance on the cowards of politicians and soldiers who had brought him to this pass, while his wife and daughter wept and were consoled by strangers, unable to avert their gaze from the death throes of their faithful servant.

There was no going on by car, so we resolved to walk the rest of the way – twenty minutes, or thirty in this heat, I predicted to myself, for this was very much my home territory.

Relieved to be out of the car, I lit a cigarette and hurried to catch Roland, who was already striding ahead.

'Does you no good, that,' he said with a glance in my direction as I caught up with him. 'You'll have no wind by the time you're my age.'

I changed the subject. 'I thought that was a promising lead – a breakthrough even – back there, but I don't see how we can follow it up with Commissaire Six's lot involved.'

'Watch me,' he said, then, 'Was there something he wasn't telling us, do you think?'

'Do you?'

'Plenty, I reckon – we'll see.'

We walked a little way, skirting the plateau Beaubourg, where extensive demolition had yet to give rise to the promised new development, creating a handy parking lot for the traders in Les Halles. Soon we were nearing the blackened walls and towers of Église Saint-Merry on my own street.

'What we do,' he said, 'is that we run a normal investigation, following every lead, checking everything, missing nothing. It's business as usual, Jojo, never mind Commissaire Six and his spooks.'

It was past seven when we reached La Salle en Haut, and a young woman in a low-cut black dress was already pouring a glass of beer for some red-bearded brute in shirtsleeves, with the thick neck and forearms of a market porter or docker. Her customer moved off as we approached and sat sipping his beer on a stool at the far end of the bar, eyeing us with distaste from time to time.

'Would you be Louise?' I asked the bartender.

She stood with her hands resting on the edge of the bar in front of her. A pleasant enough looking girl, her tawny hair loosely pinned back, a black silk choker with a rather old-fashioned cameo at the throat. I couldn't name it but there was an elusive familiarity about her.

She laughed, her widely spaced hazel eyes sparkling. Her gaze was somewhat unfocused, giving her the charming air of an ingénue; but perhaps she was merely short-sighted, and too vain to wear glasses.

'Of course it's me,' she said, 'don't you remember me, Inspector?'

I was aware of Roland's eyes on me.

'Louise Mulot? I used to work in the cloakroom at Ciao Ciao, where your Ammarah sings... She's so wonderful,' she said wistfully. 'I wish I had a voice like hers.'

I remembered her now, but the act of remembering felt unrelated to the fleeting, fugitive sense of recognition I had experienced at first sight of her.

'Could we have a word with you, mademoiselle?' Roland interrupted our little reunion. 'We need some information about Monsieur Thomas Fabricant – I believe you know him well?'

'The boss said you'd be coming in,' she said, frowning in sudden anxiety. 'Tommy's not in trouble, is he?'

'He has nothing to fear from us,' Roland replied truthfully. 'Perhaps we could talk in the office? I'm sure Monsieur Rospeau won't mind tending the bar for a while.'

'Not at all, not at all,' said Rospeau, all smiles now, emerging from the door at her back, where he had clearly been listening. 'Make yourselves at home. Drinks?'

17

The poor girl sobbed when Roland broke the news to her.

'He was a bastard to me in the end, but I did love him... such a lovely man, so kind, so gentle, so handsome... just lovely.'

She had thought he would come back to her eventually – if only she could determine what, or who, had taken him away from her so abruptly in the first place; what she had done wrong. But that would never happen now, and she began to weep again, quietly into her handkerchief.

Roland sent me to get her a glass of cognac, and when I returned with it she began to talk. Her Tommy had been a man of dark moods – never violent but often silent and inaccessible to her – and then he would snap out of it and seem to find comfort in her generous warmth, her welcoming body.

He had bad dreams, too, when he would writhe and thrash about in his sleep and sometimes shout aloud. Once or twice she had woken to find him prowling the bedroom and delving into drawers and corners, apparently conducting a thorough search while still asleep.

'What would he shout?' I asked.

'Nothing I could understand – foreign talk. He wasn't French by birth, you see, though you'd hardly know it to hear him speak.'

And how he could speak when the mood took him – politics, religion, history, science, the books she must read, all far above her head – but never about himself, never about his past. That was a book he opened for no one.

'Do you have any idea of his country of birth?' Roland asked. 'Did you think you might have recognised the language he spoke in his sleep, perhaps?'

She shook her head, a bewildered look about her. Roland waited for a beat or two and moved on.

'These bad dreams and dark moods – was Tommy afraid of something... someone?'

'Tommy? Afraid? You should see him at the door when there's trouble. I've seen him face down men threatening him with knives. He'll throw out anyone who's causing trouble, even the worst gangster you've ever heard of... And there was the time a guy turned up drunk, with a gun, threatening to shoot everyone in the place if his girl wouldn't come home to him.'

An artless pride in the strength and courage of her erstwhile lover shone in her eyes.

'Did he have any enemies, then, anyone who would wish him harm?'

She thought about this for a long time – she owed Tommy that much.

'I suppose some of the people he'd barred or thrown out might bear a grudge,' she said doubtfully, 'and there was the politics, I suppose, but I don't really understand all that. He and his mates didn't like the communists or the Jews very much, so perhaps they didn't like him back.'

Roland glanced at me, checking my reaction, but I remained impassive.

'Tommy seems to have been a man of means, doesn't he?' He said. 'You know, plenty of money.'

'That's right,' she said, glowing with pride. 'And he was always very generous. He was good to me in that way.'

Her eyes filled with tears.

'But what work did Tommy do exactly? How did he make all this money? Not on the door in this place, for sure.'

She was fairly sure of her ground now – he worked the door here and, for a commission, arranged similar work for others, also veterans of the Foreign Legion. They did other jobs too, but she was vague on the details – security, bodyguards for the rich and famous, that kind of thing, she thought.

'And he did a lot for charity, too,' she said proudly.

'Really? He does sound like a good man. Which charity was this?'

'I don't know what it's called, but it's run by his church – he's very devout, you see.'

'I do see,' said Roland. 'Which church was this, mademoiselle?'

It was the Église de l'Immaculée Conception, in the 12th.

After we had sent the girl home with our sincere thanks and condolences, and Rospeau's grudging consent, Roland used the office telephone to call Nevin, who was still toiling away at '36'. Their conversation was a short one. At the end of it, Roland sat back in the leathery depths of the swivel chair ('I had it brought over from America,' Rospeau had boasted, 'the best that money can buy.') and extracted a new pencil from his inside pocket.

Tapping his teeth with the blunt end, he said, 'All Foreign Legion records have been put out of reach – destroyed, burnt or blown up, for all we're allowed to know.'

I absorbed this disappointment and we sat in silence for several minutes, thinking.

'You know,' I said eventually. 'That's not really a surprise – there were a hell of a lot of Germans in the

78

Legion. You wouldn't want the Gestapo to get hold of their records.'

'Germans, Russians, Italians, Czechs, Poles, Spanish republicans, English... Which were you, Tommy?' Roland mused. 'Crack of dawn tomorrow, Jojo, it's holy mass for us.'

'That'll be a first,' I said, lighting a cigarette.

18

The church was a solid chunk of nineteenth century masonry crammed into a corner on rue du Rendez-Vous. Mass was already under way, a droning affair accompanied by much wafting of incense and the occasional ringing of a handbell – perhaps to keep everyone present awake, for the sparse congregation seemed to consist almost exclusively of elderly, black-clad women.

The theatrical business with the incense and the bell was managed with stern self-assurance and a stage actor's mastery of timing by a small boy in a spotless white robe, beside whom the young priest looked no more than a somewhat older and more excitable brother.

We sat quietly at the back, Roland upright and impassively following the ceremony, while I reflected on the ironic likelihood that I was the only person present, apart from the priest, who understood his ill-spoken Latin phrases.

As the old women crept forward to kneel with bowed heads at the feet of the young man, I averted my gaze for shame. To me – in this, at least, the true heir of my father – all religion seemed a repugnant renunciation of responsibility, an abdication from honesty and dignity. But I was still young, and not yet inclined to brood too much on solitude, suffering and death.

I occupied myself by looking around, counting the concrete columns masquerading as marble (six on each side), until my eye was arrested by the many candles flickering on a little altar beside the south wall and, above this, a memorial to the men of the parish killed in the last war. I conducted a rough count – close to three hundred names I calculated, from this one small city parish. No wonder the motherland had displayed so little appetite for the current conflict.

The service came to an end at last, and we waited for the priest to respond to our signal that we wished to talk. He was a thin, dark-haired young man with almond eyes and pale, translucent skin which reminded me of the martyrs who populate so many devotional paintings.

'You are policemen, I find,' he said. His accent did not belong anywhere in the Hexagon, but where then? 'Come for a little glass with me in the presbytery, and we shall discover how I may help you.'

'You are English, Father?' I ventured as he led us to his quarters.

'With a name like Aloysius Michael Kinsella, I most surely am not,' he said, laughing. 'I am a citizen of what we are no longer to call the Free State of Ireland, for my sins.' He assumed what I immediately understood to be a mock-didactic air, 'Now, the perfidious English call me Kin*sell*a and here I am known as Kinsell*a*, but you will note that, to myself and all Irish people I am, and always will be, Father Aloysius *Kin*sella. But you will certainly forget this...' He sighed a profoundly comical sigh.

He sat us down in his dark, austere little parlour and had the housekeeper place a bottle of whiskey, three tumblers and a jug of water on the little round table between us. We gratefully accepted his offer of a glass, 'To set you up for the day' – these were difficult times – and the three of us raised a toast to the freedom of Ireland and the salvation of France.

'Now,' he said, sighing as the warmth of the spirit flowed through him, 'how can I help you, gentlemen?'

Roland set his glass – barely sipped, I noted – on the table before him.

'Father, I believe your parish does a good deal of charitable work?'

'Such is our duty in Christ and, in all our vanity, our pleasure.'

'What does it involve?'

Father Kinsella smiled and thought for a few moments, turning his nearly emptied tumbler in his hands.

'How much do you know about the zone?' he asked, peering down into the glass as though he anticipated a miraculous refill.

'I know enough to expect trouble whenever we go there,' Roland replied.

The zone was a strip of land, a couple of hundred metres wide, which encircled Paris along the line of the long-since demolished defensive fortifications. The erection of buildings, and even the planting of trees, had been prohibited in order to permit defenders of the city a clear line of fire at any enemy force, a killing zone.

But the efficacy of this defensive disposition was never tested. Instead, following the reconstruction of the city centre by Baron Haussmann under the Second Empire, many poor city-dwellers were displaced and an insalubrious shanty town sprang up in the zone. Pockets of this improvised settlement remained, despite efforts over the previous forty years to suppress and clear it.

'Then you should pay more attention, if I might say so,' the priest said, smiling even as he watched to see that his point had hit home. 'There is petty crime – and sometimes worse – there, and drunkenness, yes, and every species of human folly but most of all there is misery and despair.

'There we find refugees and outcasts, the mad and the incapable, and those who have simply been unfortunate; the poorest of the poor. It is a stain on our conscience, a place of profound darkness in our famous City of Light, and we know because of his example that it

82

is precisely there to which Our Lord would direct his footsteps if he arrived in Paris today.

'So that is where we work – beyond the Porte de Vincennes, where the invisible people live on their little strip of land.'

The work, he revealed, consisted of the distribution of gifts of food and clothing, classes for children and illiterate or non-French-speaking adults, and a medical centre run by nuns and a volunteer doctor – 'A most singular individual, he is too.'

He set his glass carefully on a cork coaster on the polished table. 'Would you like to see for yourselves the condition of the people and the work we try to do?'

'Perhaps we would, at that,' said Roland. 'We've heard that a man named Thomas Fabricant, an ex-legionnaire, helps your charitable work in some way.'

'Thomas? Indeed he does. He assists our good doctor in the medical centre once a week - even Dr Descoups is moved to sing his praises. Thomas is not in any trouble, is he?'

'Do you think he might be?'

'No, he is a good man but... you are here, are you not?'

'Father, I'm afraid we bring bad news,' said Roland. 'Thomas Fabricant was murdered on Monday evening. We're trying to trace his connections so that we can find out why, and by whom.'

If it were possible, the priest grew still more pale.

'The man on the Métro?'

Somehow, everyone knew about the murder on the Métro, even though the leaflet that passed for a newspaper in these days had been prohibited from mentioning it for fear of stoking the fifth column panic.

Roland nodded. The priest crossed himself and, closing his eyes, sat for a few moments in silent prayer.

Recovering his composure, he met Roland's placid gaze and asked, 'You wouldn't have a cigarette about you, Commissaire?'

I leaned forward to offer an organ pipe array of cigarettes in my pack, lighting his selection for him.

'I had the impression, it's true, that Thomas led a rather complicated life,' said Father Kinsella.

'Complicated?'

'The parts did not all fit, if you know what I mean. He seemed to abide in many compartments, which he never allowed to mix.'

'Were you his confessor, Father?'

The priest's dark, good-humoured eyes darted, their gaze coming to rest on Roland's solid, impassive face.

'Now, Commissaire, you know better than to ask a question like that,' he said with the trace of a smile.

'Ever heard of the Chevaliers de la France Catholique, Father?' Roland asked casually.

Father Kinsella held his gaze but the smile withered on his lips and his brow furrowed as he sucked angrily on his cigarette. Suddenly he looked much older.

'As I said, Thomas's life was complicated, and its pieces didn't always seem to make a whole, if you catch my drift. I know of his links to that group, but in his work with us there was never the slightest suggestion of their evil ideology. That they dare to associate themselves with the name of Christ's own house!'

'Did he speak of them with you?'

'I can say no more on the matter. As I said already, Thomas's life was complicated.'

Roland nodded to indicate that he understood, but I felt we were skating over something vital, perhaps because these two men wished to save my feelings.

'What, exactly, is the ideology of this group?' I asked.

The commissaire sighed, softly for such a big man, but the little priest spoke fearlessly since I had asked the question.

'They hold that republican France is irredeemably decadent and has been emasculated by the malign influence – I am sorry, Inspector – of the Jew; and that the church in France is riddled with what they call 'liberal sentimentalism' and has ceased to stand firm for what they regard as Christian virtues. They seek national and religious 'renewal' through revolution and the creation of a state modelled upon Hitler's Germany under a restored monarchy.'

How could this young Irishman tell, I wondered. Was it so obvious? Was it written upon my person in some way? If what Roland had said about the nature of the Nazi regime was true, what were my chances? Perhaps I should have followed his advice and got out.

But no. This was my city, and always would be, as it had been my father's before me and his before him. I would stay. No matter what.

'In fact,' Father Kinsella continued, 'they go further and advocate the complete and final removal of Jews from France, if necessary by their annihilation.'

'And Thomas believed this? Was a militant in this cause?'

I struggled vainly to reconcile this intelligence – the implicit likelihood made explicitly true – with Kinsella's description of him as 'a good man.'

'He was complicated,' he repeated, 'and not always easy to read but I do not care to imagine that he believed any such thing.'

'But we must follow the trail wherever it leads us,' Roland said, I think to reassure me, perhaps to reassert his own resolve. 'We'll go to the zone with you, Father, if you'll take us.'

85

19

Father Kinsella conducted us through deserted sunlit streets towards the zone and his mission. On the corner of rue Marsoulan, a newspaper vendor had but one paper to sell, and that a nugatory sheet entitled Edition Parisienne de Guerre, No 1. Men over seventeen and not employed in essential services were ordered to leave the city, I noted at a glance. Defeat and humiliation – and perhaps something worse – were closing in on us.

'Tell me, Father,' Roland was saying, 'do you know everyone in the zone just here, beyond the Porte de Vincennes?'

'I certainly know of everybody.'

'We came across a couple who were just moving out – Jewish, Czech...'

'Ah, so, you mean the Lederers – a fine woman she is, but born to suffer bravely, it would appear.'

Alfred Lederer, Father Kinsella told us, lacked the conspicuous fortitude of his wife. Humiliated to find himself exiled to a filthy hovel in a foreign land where he possessed no working knowledge of the language, he had succumbed to despair and to spite.

His wife worked, how she worked – as a cleaner, as a waitress, as a walker of fat little dogs for wealthy, and very thin, old women – and he sent her to spend the money she earned on the cheap wine in which he sought comfort every day, never leaving the miserable confines of the hut they shared. And when she returned to him after work he would subject her to ranting accusations of infidelity, and on bad days a beating. In the zone, they were far from unique, the priest concluded with a shake of the head.

I thought about the apparently affectionate couple I had seen on the platform at Saint-Paul and then interviewed at 36. They had certainly been skilled in concealing their secret torment, and the man with whom I had spoken in Yiddish had not corresponded to any naïve notion of a wife-beater.

However, a few years service in the police teaches anyone capable of learning that there is no 'type' of man who batters his wife or rapes his daughters. The depressing truth is that any man could turn out to be such a brute, from the drunk who brawls in the street to your dour and prudent bank manager, or the brilliant surgeon who saved your life. One must keep an open mind, assume nothing.

'This doctor,' Roland was saying to Father Kinsella, 'you implied he's a bit of an odd fellow – what's his name?'

'Ah yes, our Dr Ferdinand-Auguste Descoups,' said the priest, looking straight ahead. 'He has, I believe, something of a second career as a novelist and pamphleteer under the name...'

'Cassandre! I know him.'

Roland addressed me, evidently not minding that Father Kinsella could also hear.

'We hauled him in back in '37, suspicion of involvement in the Cagoule business – the stuff he'd written was so full of hate that some of it was banned – but it turned out he hated them too. Bunch of thugs and pansies, he said; couldn't run a birthday party, never mind a revolution, he said. So we had to let him go.'

'Yes,' said Father Kinsella, 'poor Descoups has a formidable lot of hating going on, all right. What is it? Communists, socialists, liberals, democrats...'

'Conservatives, freemasons, homosexuals, protestants...' added Roland.

87

'He's not too keen on us Catholics either, mind, and the English, the Americans, Arabs...'

'Blacks, the poor, women, and most of all...'

'The Jews, of course,' I interjected, sure of my ground. 'Always the Jews.'

'I was going to say the French, because he reckons they were weak and womanish enough to let the Jews get away with it,' Roland said. 'He's a piece of work and no mistake.'

'And yet, strangely,' said Kinsella, 'he's been a good doctor to these people, most of them belonging to one or more of the groups he professes to despise. Perhaps God has found a way to his heart...'

'He ain't got one,' said Roland, lapsing into the crude dialect of his origins in the Pas-de-Calais.

'I can't wait to meet him,' I said.

20

To pass from the ordered intramural streets into the zone was to step from the most effervescent and cultured city in modern Europe, the city of light, back to the earliest days of humanity, when our unfortunate ancestors dwelt in dirt and darkness and weather; and disease, hunger, ignorance and violence prevailed.

As if news of our imminent arrival had carried before us like some taint on the air, the narrow muddy tracks that meandered between the settlement's incredible assortment of dwellings had been deserted by all but a bold handful of grubby, ragged children who called and capered in our wake like a pack of juvenile baboons.

By way of contrast, the animal life of the zone, unperturbed by our presence, persisted in its own routines. Lean dogs slunk along between unsound walls, a row of insolent cats eyed us from atop a crude, clinker-built fence, pigeons popped their heads out of their roosts in a cote improvised from what appeared to be a pyramid of lobster baskets, and a mottled pig rooted among the stink of a mountainous midden.

A group of three gipsy caravans sat side by side, with no horses anywhere to be seen, and alongside them a hut built of corrugated asbestos with an upper floor of timber implausibly balanced upon its fragile roof. In the yard at the back of a shack crudely assembled from an amazing miscellany of bricks, timber and stones, three women sat before heaps of ash and rubbish, picking and sorting rags, glass and stale crusts into separate baskets. Behind them a patched cauldron steamed on a trivet, giving off the barbarous stink of boiled bones.

An elderly man in a greasy beret which shaded his eyes and slackly drooped to cover his ears into the bargain was standing in a wooden barrel a quarter filled with water, wielding a heavy pole and pounding for all he was worth at the armfuls of paper flung at his feet by a mournful child with cold sores. From a similar barrel filled with paper already beaten to a pulp a sickly lass – a greenish tint about her complexion – was pouring, packing and smoothing the material into a grid of wooden frames, each about the size of a housebrick.

'Chiffoniers,' said Father Kinsella in answer to my puzzled expression. 'Nothing remotely serviceable will go to waste – see this family here have their own little manufacturing enterprise, making bricks of wastepaper compacted with glue to burn in the hearths of Paris. Dry these, paint them with a smear of paraffin, take a barrowload out to sell on the streets and they might eat for another day.'

'It looks like terribly hard work,' I said lamely.

Shame burned within me – that old man still pounding away like a navvy, the poor, near-naked child, the girl who looked at death's door; consumptive I supposed.

'Terrible hard work it is. Living is terrible hard work, did you and I but know it. Every day, these people save Paris from suffocating beneath her own refuse. Did you not know?'

I asked him if he knew which of these appalling hovels had housed the Lederers, and he pointed without comment to the end of a fetid impasse where a shelter of sorts had been assembled from corrugated iron, crates and billboards with a sheet of tarpaulin for a roof.

The privilege of tenancy had evidently passed already to new occupants, for on the threshold a tattooed Berber woman, her back bent double under the twin burdens of age and extreme poverty, fought with improvised hazel besom in hands a valiant but doomed battle with dust.

Father Kinsella's clinic was a modest single-storey structure in rendered brick, box-like and functional in design, though in these surroundings it might have passed for the Taj Mahal or the doge's palace. A young nun, her sweetly freckled face framed by a wimple, sat behind a desk and looked up with a welcoming smile as we entered.

Seeing the priest, she stood abruptly, scattering index cards all around her.

'Father, it is you. I, we...'

'It is I, indeed it is, sister, or so it was the last time I checked. Will you sit down now, and let me collect your papers together.'

He knelt at her feet and reassembled the cards, handing them up to her with a smile. She blushed, almost too flustered to know how to accept them from his hands.

'Is he in?' he asked.

He was in and, at first sight, Dr Descoups was not at all what I was expecting. A meagre little fellow of disturbingly handsome countenance – a head of wiry black hair coming to a pronounced widow's peak, the hollow cheeks of a romantic hero, and full lips with the slightest suggestion of a cynical curl at the edges – leapt up from his seat behind a desk as Father Kinsella opened the door for us.

A gitane sent up a coiling smokescreen from a full ash-tray on his desk, and the uncapped fountain pen in his left hand suggested that he had been interrupted in the act of writing. I wondered what message he had for the world today, but it seemed he had only been making an entry in his last patient's notes.

'Tertiary syphilis,' he said to nobody in particular. 'Poor fucker.'

The voice was grating and vulgar, quite unlike that of any doctor I had ever encountered.

'I know you,' he said to Roland.

'We have met,' Roland acknowledged.

'I had the impression that we'd said everything that we could possibly have to say to each other,' said Descoups, almost snarling.

'I'll let you know the moment that's so, doctor,' replied Roland without a trace of resentment.

'Well, I'll be off and about my business,' Father Kinsella said hastily, 'now that you have renewed each other's acquaintance, you know.'

The doctor and the commissaire, locked in mutual contempt, made no comment on his leaving.

'How's your mission to save France from herself going these days, doctor?'

Descoups wagged a tobacco-stained finger at the commissaire and stepped forward until he peered up at him, much as a man might take the measure of a mountain before commencing its conquest.

'France? France? What did I tell you? France has failed to wipe its own fucking arse, and now the Germans will have to do it for us,' he said with evident relish.

'May I introduce my colleague, Inspector Saint-Simon?' said Roland with a courtly gesture.

Saint-Simon: the adaptation of my name a signal that something abhorrent was sniffing the air and liable to make its move.

'Saint-Simon, you say?' The doctor regarded me with a wolfish leer.

I became aware of a smell in the room, some primal musk beneath the familiar odours of tobacco smoke, clinical disinfectant and sweat.

I returned his gaze steadily and nodded, 'Good morning, Dr Descoups.'

Like a man driven by an irresistible impulse, he took up the threads of his theme.

'I told you – the cowards and the stinking swine of the so-called Third Republic, all they were interested in was snouts in the trough. As long as they got their grub, as long as they were taken up the Tour d'Argent weekly [I suspected an allusion to sodomy here] by their Jewboy paymasters, they couldn't give a fuck. The rest – the nation, the race, European fucking civilisation – could fall into ruins and enslavement. It's happened before and it's happening now. But believe me, these Germans know what they're doing, what they're up against, and they'll put a stop to it.'

'Put a stop to what, doctor?' Roland spoke mildly.

The doctor threw himself into his chair and reached for the pack of gitanes. 'Mongrelisation, enslavement, the ruin of the culture, of everything that's fine and civilised.'

He made a large gesture which I took to encompass Shakespeare, Mozart, Flaubert, Proust... Perhaps not Proust, born of a Jewish mother.

'But who's responsible for all this?' asked Roland.

I was watching him closely. His florid features had paled with anger but he maintained a dogged calmness of manner.

Descoups drew deeply on his cigarette and watched Roland through the writhing coils of smoke, smirking with contempt.

'Who? The Jew, of course. Who else controls two-thirds of this country's wealth?'

Without so much as a sidelong glance at me, Roland, his forehead creased as in perplexity, quietly replied, 'You seem to rate these Jews pretty high, monsieur. I reckon most of the Jews I've met are cobblers and carpenters, or tinsmiths and the like. My barber's a Jew, I think. Does he secretly control millions? Is he quietly planning to cut my throat while he gives me his hopeless racing tips and tells me another dirty joke? And you say a few thousand of these israélites are going to enslave god knows how many million Frenchmen and women? How does that work, then?'

He shook his great head in a mighty admission of incomprehension.

Descoups spoke through his teeth, 'The power of Will, a conspiracy centuries in the making.'

'Well, Monsieur, you make them sound absolutely first-rate, like some kind of a master race, doesn't he, Saint-Simon?'

Too stunned to reply, I managed to purse my lips, conveying doubt.

'Well, it's a point of view,' Roland continued, 'that it is. It's a point of view, all right.'

Descoups laughed, provoking a bout of coughing. When he recovered he sat back in his chair and looked at us both, not unfriendly.

'You think I'm barking mad, don't you. Well, it has been said, but you'll see – just watch the Germans when they get here. But you didn't come here for a nice little political chat, did you, commissaire? One of my flock here been misbehaving?'

'Actually,' I said, 'we'd like to talk to you about Thomas Fabricant.'

21

News of the death of Thomas Fabricant abruptly stemmed the torrent of words and opinions that had been swirling angrily around us. The doctor sat in silence and smoked, motionless and suddenly frail. We took seats across the desk from him and waited.

Finally, he spoke: 'He was a good lad, Thomas, and would have made a fine physician.'

Then, after lighting a second cigarette: 'He was a cretin for involving himself with those arseholes – I told him so.'

'Which arseholes?' asked Roland.

'What do the morons call themselves... Les Chevaliers de la France Catholique? I ask you – did you ever hear anything so fucking absurd?'

The words remained harsh but the tone of his voice had smoothed and softened. It occurred to me that he had been genuinely fond of Thomas.

'He was good to have around, that boy. Do you know, when the priest first brought him to me, I thought, ohoh, another one of your reformed fucking hardmen looking for redemption (I rather think our Aloysius has a certain penchant for that type, if you understand me) but that wasn't it at all.'

'When was this?' Roland laid the question down lightly between them, hardly seeming to interrupt at all.

'A few months ago, certainly after war was declared, say the turn of the year? The thing was, the boy had learning, technical ability. I could trust him to help with the patients – it wasn't just a matter of him coming in to tidy up around me, or set to with a mop and fucking bucket.'

With a wave of the hand he drew attention to the condition of the room, which was, in fact, with the deplorable exception of the surface of his desk, impeccable – shelves of medicine jars, an examination couch covered with a sheet of virginal white, a trolley on which a white towel covered the instruments of his craft. All was neat, shining, perfectly clean and aseptic.

'I often asked him about it – where he'd learned all this – but he always tried to fob me off with a heap of horse shit about first aid training in the Legion. I'd say "bollocks" but he'd just smile and shrug and say that's how it was. Then one day we went for a drink or two and he told me.

'He'd been a medical student, got too involved with a girl whose family wanted his head for a doorstop, and ran off to join the Foreign Legion – some idiocy about reading 'Beau Geste' in the original English. I don't know why a bright kid like him would bother with that kind of shit – I told him, if you want to read English, Conrad's your man...' He smirked bitterly, 'I suppose he'd have run away to the British Merchant Marine if he'd read Conrad.'

Descoup's scorn for the youthful dreams of glory which had, by an indirect route, led our victim to an ignominious end deep beneath the streets of a foreign city awoke in me a potent fellow-feeling for the young Thomas.

I well remembered the feel, the look, the smell of the Détective magazines, so avidly feasted upon, that had inspired in me the determination to follow in the footsteps of the greats of the Police Judiciaire, whose exploits filled the weekly's pages. Indeed, it was in my bedroom, reading by torchlight beneath the covers, that I had first encountered the name and the legend of Inspector Arthur Roland of the PJ.

'Did you ask where he was from, where he'd studied medicine?' Roland asked.

'Of course I did, but he was very cagey about that, wouldn't let on.'

'What did you think, though? You must have had some ideas.'

He shrugged and lit another gitane, 'Not German, not English, not mediterranean. Look East, I'd say – Poland, Austria, Hungary, Bohemia... Romania even.'

Roland accepted that he was not going to get any tighter identification, in terms of our man's origin.

'You knew about him and this political group, so you did discuss politics.'

'Politics? Me? What do you think? Yes, we discussed politics, but the mob he was involved with... hardly qualifies as political in any serious or sane world view.'

That was rich coming from him, I thought.

'Plenty of money behind them,' he continued, 'but the politics is fantasy stuff – unicorns and ends of the rainbow shit... Nasty though, very nasty.'

This made my ears prick up – I could hardly bring myself to imagine a political project considered 'nasty' by this character.

'You know them?' Roland toyed gently with the brim of his hat in his lap.

'Yes, I know them. They thought they could bring me on board with them, but I told them where they could shove it – ponces, madmen and bullshitters the lot of them.'

'You said you told Thomas he was an idiot to mix with these people...'

'A cretin, I told him he was a cretin but he just shrugged and laughed in that way of his. Perhaps it was the money, perhaps he thought he could make enough to go back home and get his girl, I don't know – it made no sense. It still makes no sense.'

Roland allowed him some time to think.

'Unless... No, not him.'

Roland nodded, agreeing to dismiss some unspoken speculation that lay between them.

'Could they have killed him, do you think?'

Descoups snorted in derision and lit another cigarette, even though the last one still smouldered in the ash tray.

'Those handkerchief-clutching vinegar-pissers? I doubt it, but I suppose it's just about possible if they lost trust in him, thought he'd betrayed them – they've got muscle available, ex-army types, he was evidence of that himself.'

'Tell me about them, everything you know.'

'Monarchists with a twist. The arse they want to plant on the throne belongs, they say, to some character known personally to only one of them, who has a proven pedigree going back to the Merovingians, to Clovis himself.

'Religious maniacs, militarists, nativists, colonialists, again with a twist. They think of themselves as the New Crusaders. Not only insane but historically fucking ignorant. Idiotic schoolboys!'

'What do you know about this pretender to the throne?'

'Nothing. They call him the Duc d'Éden, can you believe it? Perhaps he doesn't exist.'

'You said they're colonialists with a twist,' I could not help but intervene. 'What's the twist?'

He drew deeply on his cigarette, staring at me insolently.

'Ah, you're awake are you? I'd wondered – wide awake and got a voice all of your own. Well, so far as I can make sense of their incoherent rantings, they're proposing a combination of slave labour and mass slaughter in the colonies. Perhaps their fantasy duke is

98

the reincarnation of good old Leopold of Belgium and the Congo.

'Oh, and there's talk of forcibly deporting the Jews to Madagascar... or worse. I told them I'd have no truck with colonialism of any kind. France for the Frenchman and Africa for the African is the first principle.

'As for the israélite... What is to be done? And where? Where does the homeless wanderer, the universal trickster fit, I wonder?'

Roland gave me a look that told me to slip my notebook discreetly from my pocket and prepare myself to take notes.

'Names, Monsieur; names and addresses.'

'With pleasure. You know about Rue Mesnil? Well, don't bother with that place – just a barrack room for the bully-boys, and panelled boardrooms where their betters get together to get pissed and share their infantile fucking pipe-dreams. No, if I were you, I'd go straight to the top. You want Victor, the Comte de l'Île or, at a pinch, his sidekick who's something high up in the Ministry of Finance... what's his name now... De Nouailles, that's it.'

I couldn't restrain myself.

'Julien De Nouailles?'

Roland and I exchanged glances. His glance instructed me to shut up.

'That's him. You know him? Is he a person of interest? That fat fop?'

'I met him once,' I improvised unconvincingly.

Descoups stared through me, smirking unpleasantly.

'No,' he said, 'go and speak to old Victor – I've an idea Thomas worked as the old fraud's bodyguard when required. I'd love to see the look on his pansy aristocratic face when you tread your muck into his Persian fucking carpet.'

He gave an address on Quai de Bourbon on the Île Saint-Louis.

The door opened and the young nun peered in, blinking nervously. Over her shoulder I saw that the waiting room had filled with as pitiable an assortment of humanity as might be found in any of the most pestilential slums of the world, and among them the bent old Berber woman.

As we were taking our leave, the doctor stood in the doorway and glanced around the bowed heads of the waiting crowd, assessing who stood in most urgent need of his services.

'Goodbye, Commissaire,' he cried as he advanced purposefully on the old woman.

I hesitated on the threshold, half-expecting a need to rush to her defence, but she smiled up at him as he took her gently by the hand and spoke to her softly as he led her into his consulting room.

'Come, mother, let us change those dressings and, next time, don't make yourself struggle all the way over here – I keep telling you, I shall come to you.'

She smiled up at him, open-mouthed and toothless, and said something that I couldn't hear. Perhaps she was telling him that she'd moved home.

He smiled pleasantly in return.

'How's that great big son of yours, eh? Found a job yet?'

Our eyes met briefly and he shrugged and smiled and turned back to his patient before the door closed behind them.

In that moment I understood that he was, indeed, quite mad, a self divided by an incessant internal war between pity and contempt. But perhaps I misjudged him and the two sentiments are not so much at variance after all.

22

The order had gone out to round up all the stray dogs, but here came a pack of all shapes, sizes and colours: a loping hound, two scurrying terriers, a black retriever, a miniature white poodle, its perm growing out, and a couple of street-wise mongrels. How such a disparate band recognised each other as fellow dogs was a mystery to me.

They swaggered across Pont Marie until, arriving at a spot with some acceptable combination of sun and shade, they came to a unanimous resolution to flop down and rest. They watched us as we passed, some with indifference, some only too clearly craving human attention; reproach and entreaty in their moist brown eyes.

Otherwise, the mid-day streets were deserted. The city held its breath and waited, for now oppressed only by a terrible silence.

In this baleful atmosphere it seemed absurd that the Métro was still running on time, ferrying its few remaining pilgrims across the suffering city as though between the stations of the cross. But a Line 1 train had reliably scooped us up at Porte de Vincennes and deposited us at Saint-Paul with the same mechanical efficiency as ever, as if no human agency was involved at all.

The white stone façade of the Hôtel de l'Île on Quai de Bourbon gleamed among its soot-blackened neighbours like the solitary good tooth in a set long neglected and decayed. Someone cared greatly about appearances.

The high oaken gates stood open, tended only by a sheepish fourteen-year-old attired in a ludicrous pastiche of the livery of an ancien régime footman – a blue jacket with gold trimmings, white hose, and even a powdered wig. Several cars were parked haphazardly in the courtyard behind him, among them a late model Delahaye, as hot and rare as a dragon's breath.

'Invitations only,' squeaked the youth, raising a thin, pale hand to stop us.

'Good, here's mine,' said Roland, flourishing the commission rogatoire in the startled lad's face. 'Now, where do we find your boss?'

'The Comte? You're here to see the Comte?'

The adam's apple rattled up and down his scrawny neck. He seemed unable to swallow our barefaced presumption, and was no doubt calculating the likely effect of our unwanted intrusion on his prospects of continued employment.

I stepped forward and placed a paternal hand on his bony, gold-braided shoulder.

'Good lad, you've got it. Now, where is he?'

'He, he's holding a salon.' A wavering finger pointed to the heavens. 'First floor, f-front, in the big drawing room...the green room. But there's all sorts of very important people there...'

'They must be the last ones left in Paris then,' Roland remarked affably. 'Don't worry, son, we won't mind them if they don't mind us. Come on, Jojo.'

Roland forged his implacable way through the grand house, sweeping aside the puny interventions of household retainers, with me coasting in his wake. I am no follower of sport but I had a sudden sense of the awe it must have inspired to see this titan of the rugby field in action, trampling and scattering all before him.

The instantly recognisable singing voice of a fashionable chansonnier accompanied us to the door of the green room, and there he was, René Vidal himself at the piano, surrounded by female admirers in various assemblages of charmeuse and chiffon, singing his latest, not entirely unironic, anthem to rural France. Something to do with a pike and a poacher, if I recall correctly.

Most of the men – I recognised a couple of right-wing deputies, the editor of a popular conservative newspaper, and the celebrated author of thinly-veiled antisemitic polemics – stood in a semi-circle near a window overlooking the Seine, respectfully listening to the quietly impassioned speech of the elderly man who faced them, gripping tightly the back of the green and gilt rococo chair before him as he spoke. A bashful young woman in a green and gold chinois tunic loitered nearby with a tray full of champagne glasses.

The walls of the room were papered with hand-painted images of climbing plants – ivy, jasmine, vines, clematis and honeysuckle – and hung with oils of nymphs and shepherds getting up to their usual capers. On the floor was an immense Persian carpet, emerald green with gold arabesques, and ancien régime furniture, all gold touches and candy twirls, stood in groups about the place as if it only awaited the word.

A woman of about thirty – blonde, a real beauty draped in silks and pearls – lounged on a chaise longue at the far end of the room, beneath a huge canvas depicting the trial of Jeanne d'Arc, the English looking a ripe set of creeps and villains. Inexplicably, in the hand that did not hold a Havana cigar, she negligently dangled a dog's lead, at the other end of which a tiger cub kept hungry vigil over a nearby sideboard laden with cold meats and patisseries.

Silencing the liveried flunkey at the door with a glare and a flash of his police badge, Roland loudly declared our presence.

'Victor, le Comte de l'Île?'

The room fell silent and all eyes turned to discover the source of this impertinence. I noticed that none of the men's eyes quite met Roland's steady gaze, while the women and Monsieur Vidal, sensing the animal force of his unselfconscious masculinity, regarded him with a hungry, yet wary fascination.

'I am Commissaire Arthur Roland of the police judiciaire and I wish to speak with Monsieur le Comte, if he would identify himself,' Roland said into the silence.

The old man beside the window straightened his back and spoke above the heads of his erstwhile listeners.

'I am he.'

23

The count's refined features were drawn tight with fury.

'Explain yourselves,' he demanded.

He had silently conducted us to a study overlooking the courtyard, and stood with his back to the window so that we saw him only in silhouette. Sighing, Roland eased himself into a chair, signalling that I should do likewise. Here all was polished dark wood, morocco leather and gold; the musty smell of old money and rare books, shelves and shelves of them.

With a warning glance at me, Roland leaned forward to place the magistrate's warrant on the desk and then sat back in his chair, silent; as watchful and hungry as the inexplicable young tiger.

The old man did not so much as glance at the document.

'What the devil do you mean by invading my home?'

'Oh, I'm afraid we're all going to have to get used to that kind of thing soon enough, don't you think, monsieur?' said Roland, eliciting a spasm of annoyance from our unwilling host.

He was a tall man, straight-backed for his age, and thin, almost spectral with the light behind him – my father would have called him an extreme ectomorph. Beneath the long, aristocratic nose his lips seemed permanently puckered, as though deploring the stench of the world beneath him.

'Tell us about the Chevaliers de la France Catholique,' Roland said abruptly.

'What is this nonsense? Get out of this house before I call the prefect of police and have him order you out.'

He stepped up to the desk and reached for the telephone receiver.

'Call him, monsieur, please. We can wait – our pleasure. Only, don't try to tell us that you know nothing of a group whose emblem you wear inside your lapel, just on the other end of that tiny golden pin.'

There was a knock on the door.

'Victor, my dear, will you be long? Our guests are about to leave.'

Urgent appointments elsewhere, suddenly called to mind by the unannounced arrival of the police judiciaire, no doubt. The door opened to reveal the shapely form of the mysterious blonde, now cradling the tiger cub like a baby.

'Do come and see everyone off,' she pleaded with a pout aimed in my direction. 'Darling René will be so disappointed.'

'Would you be so kind as to perform that duty for me, Marianne, my dear,' said the count. 'It seems I have important matters to discuss with these... gentlemen.'

With a disappointed moue she withdrew, closing the door behind her.

'My wife,' the old man explained unnecessarily, 'the third countess.'

We maintained a silence at once tactful and tactical.

The count folded himself into the chair across the desk from us and turned the commission rogatoire so that he could read it. Finally, with the air of a diner rejecting a suspect oyster, he pushed it away and regarded us haughtily.

'Again, I ask, what is your business with me?'

'Thomas Fabricant, once of the French Foreign Legion,' said Roland abruptly. He sat back and folded one long leg over the other, balancing the pork-pie hat on his knee.

The count's expression did not change. 'Who?'

With a nod of the head, Roland indicated that I should go and stand behind the old man. Despite himself, the count's eyes tracked my movements until I was out of his sight but standing so close that he could feel my presence. I allowed myself an idle glance down into the courtyard, where René Vidal was installing the tiger cub in the passenger seat of the red Delahaye before embracing his hostess and taking the wheel.

'Your bodyguard, Thomas, Tommy, Tom Pouce. Don't try to tell me that you don't know who I'm talking about.'

I exhaled softly, so that the old man would feel my breath on his neck. He shivered.

'All right, I know him. Of course I know him. What of it?'

'A member of your little club, or cult, or party, or gang, or whatever you like to call it, was he?'

'That is none of your business. Thomas is perfectly entitled to choose his own associations.'

'He was,' said Roland. 'We all are... for now.'

The telephone on the desk rang and the count positively scrambled to pick up the receiver.

'De l'Île,' he said, inviting us, with a wave of the hand, to leave the presence.

Roland sat watching him, a polite frown on his broad brow. The count listened for a long time, thoughtfully extracting a Sobranie from the gold case on the desk as he did so. His only contribution to the conversation was to end it.

'Thank you for informing me.'

He sat, head bowed, pensively stroking that supercilious upper lip, before appearing to make a decision.

'You might as well know,' he said, 'General Weygand has declared Paris an open city, there will be no battle of Paris.'

I did not know what to feel – relief, shame, despair? – but Roland kept his gaze on the count.

'Did you have Thomas Fabricant killed, monsieur?'

24

Victor le comte de l'Île sat deep in his chair and steepled his fingers, regarding Roland with the native indifference of an aristocrat in obligatory conversation with the man who trims his hedges.

'Of course not,' he said. 'Now will you inform me why you have intruded upon me?'

'Isn't it obvious?' I whispered into his right ear. A long transparent hair grew from it, having apparently escaped detection by his barber.

'Not to me,' he said, the irritation aroused at being addressed by an underling directed towards the commissaire. Roland might look like a farm hand but he did hold a position of some note.

'It's perfectly simple, monsieur,' said Roland in the same civil tone that he would adopt with a street-sweeper. 'Thomas Fabricant was murdered on Monday evening. We know of an association between you, and we are following all of his associations in pursuit of our inquiry. Shall we begin with the organisation to which you both belong?'

The count folded his hands on the desk in front of him, but not before his head had turned minutely, reflexively to the right, towards the bookcase on which my hand now rested. Something was there – a safe, perhaps, behind those rows of books? Behind his back I pointed to the bookcase with my thumb. Roland nodded, indifferent to the count's hostile gaze.

'The Chevaliers de la France Catholique is a perfectly legal entity...'

'Oh, it's a bit paramilitary though, isn't it, a bit over the line? We have been to Rue Mesnil, you know.'

'There are no uniforms, no marches, and no acts of violence have ever been attributed to our organisation...'

'So you're an undercover paramilitary group, biding your time, are you?' Roland probed away, trying to needle him.

'No,' the count spoke evenly but his knuckles were white, his grip tensing, 'We are a relatively new monarchist organisation, campaigning for the restitution of order in France, the restoration of the catholic faith and catholic values in public and private life, and the efficient conduct of colonial affairs.'

'Campaigning? How is it I've never heard of you? You heard of them, inspector?'

'Never,' I said from a spot close to the back of the count's head. He retained a full head of silver hair swept back somewhat in the shape of a Grecian helmet.

'I told you, we are a new organisation.'

Roland sat in silence for a few moments, appearing to give this some consideration.

'I'm not sure that I understand where you differ from Action Française and Monsieur Charles Maurras,' he said eventually.

The count relaxed and settled back into his chair. This appeared to be a matter on which he was prepared to expound.

'Maurras's catholicism, like Bonaparte's, is merely contingent, ours heartfelt; and his conception of the monarchy is flaccid and impotent, ours absolute, commanding. Charles Maurras has always sought power for his own ends, we want nothing for ourselves. '

Roland nodded appreciatively. 'I see. Thank you, monsieur.'

The count's rising resentment at the common appellation 'monsieur' was incongruously mirrored by Roland's increasingly insistent humility and placidity.

'That is good to hear,' Roland continued, smiling as though in relief. Then the sidestep: 'Tell me, who is the Duc d'Éden?'

De l'Île held up an exquisitely manicured hand. 'I cannot say anything beyond this: unlike the Orléanist pretender, His Grace has lived humbly in France throughout his life, serving his people.'

'Very well, let's move on.'

The count's hand dropped to the desk. He seemed almost disappointed by Roland's lack of interest.

'Tell me, if you would, how long had Thomas Fabricant been with you, and what duties did he perform for you and your organisation?'

The count shrugged and lit another cigarette. 'He came to us, on a recommendation, in late '38.'

'As the Cagoule was being taken down?'

The count appeared not to hear this.

'As to his duties, Fabricant could make himself useful, and was worthy of the recommendation I had received, but he was not a person of any importance.'

I had the impression that, for the count, 'importance' was an attribute restricted to the members of very few families indeed. Roland waited, forcing him to expand upon his answer.

'He was a perfectly reliable courier, a bodyguard when needed, and we occasionally called on him in the training of recruits. As I said, nothing of any great importance.'

'Did he have rivals within the organisation?'

'Rivals? I told you, he was simply not significant enough to have rivals.'

'Or might he have made enemies among the opponents of your organisation?'

'Again, I told you, we are not an organisation that engages in militancy.'

'And yet there are armed guards at your building in Rue Mesnil.'

Roland was stretching more than a little here, guessing. It was a good guess.

'Of course, we have the right to self-defence. These are extraordinary times, and who knows when the communists might strike?'

'Ah, the cocos, of course. We'll be sure to have a word with them, monsieur, if we can find them. In the meantime,' Roland gambled, 'what will we find when we ask you to open the safe behind that bookcase?'

There was nothing but bundles of cash. He must have placed his records beyond reach or destroyed them.

25

It was a hot afternoon. We took our suit jackets off and slung them over our shoulders as we crossed to the Île de la Cité and strolled along Rue du-Cloître-Notre-Dame in the shadow of the cathedral. While I smoked and indulged in pleasing fantasies featuring Ammarah, Roland plodded along silently at my side, his broad brow wrinkled in thought. I noted that he, as usual, chose not to carry a concealed weapon, and felt suddenly self-conscious about my own shoulder-holstered automatic, normally the object of secret, puerile pride.

'We are getting nowhere,' Roland said suddenly. 'Something's not right. We're not looking in the right places.'

'Oh, I don't know,' I said, flicking the cigarette butt at the mountain of sandbags protecting the sanctified walls of the cathedral. 'We now know that our victim was a one-time medical student from somewhere in east or central Europe, who ran away to join the Foreign Legion in flight from his girlfriend's family. We know that he worked for a shady club-owner and known mobster, and regularly handled his money. Whatever that mad old bastard says, we know that he was involved up to his neck in a quasi-fascist political movement. We know that he was very religious and that he did charitable work in the zone. I'd say we know quite a lot about him. The picture's definitely building.'

'But we're no nearer knowing who killed him or why. We're allowing ourselves to be sent round in circles.' He paused, looked up at the bright summer sky: 'But who by?'

'My money's on Rospeau or our new friend, the count and his people... Or, at a push, the communists.'

'Neither of them even knew he was dead before we told them, I'm sure of it. It was news to both of them, and unwelcome news at that.'

My suggestion of communist involvement was not dismissed out of hand, I noted, but neither was it supported. In truth, we both recognised that no scent of the comrades hung about this crime. They would have shot him in the back of the head as he made his way down some dark alley, or garrotted him where he sat in a restaurant booth, and they certainly wouldn't have wanted to conceal his identity. The reds wanted their little acts of revenge to be known, to serve as acts of propaganda and warning.

'I don't know,' I said. 'I'm not so sure about that. Gangsters, aristocrats, they've something in common, I'd say, when it comes to masking their true feelings.'

As we crossed the parvis of Notre Dame – the majestic gothic façade of the cathedral hidden behind stacks of sandbags, as sad a sight as that of the face of a mother veiled in mourning – Roland mused, 'Maybe the answer lies earlier in his life – in his days in the Legion, perhaps, or the girl's family catching up with him here. We just don't know enough about the background, and that door is closed to us right now.'

He puffed his cheeks in frustration, and the vibration of his lips as he exhaled caused a passing priest to jump and whinny in surprise, so closely did the sound resemble the snort of an exasperated bull about to charge.

I looked back at the cathedral as we crossed to the riverside. Here, just a few days ago, on Sunday, government and church had assembled to pray for the salvation of France. The most high, the most wealthy, the most honoured and hallowed our nation could muster had cast up their plea to the heavens for divine intervention.

114

Their call had gone unanswered. France was surely lost.

The sun shone brightly on the Quai des Orfèvres and even the green, glittering river appeared to move more languidly in the heat. In the wake of a passing barge it seemed as though the water itself had thickened and transformed into some other substance, glassy, viscous, somehow sinister, as though a terrible serpent rolled and coiled beneath, never quite breaking the surface. It was nauseating.

Inside 36, a miasma of foreboding hung in the air. People went about their business mechanically, dead-eyed and silent. Roland muttered something and entered his office, closing the door behind him. I listened for the crash as he threw himself into his long-suffering chair: the commissaire's thinking time.

I passed along the corridor towards my insalubrious shared office, merely nodding to colleagues out of respect for the prevailing mood. Through the window of the 'aquarium' I could see that Nevin was out, his neat desk primly awaiting his return. Only Clément lay sprawled in his chair, speaking on the telephone. A new notice had been pasted onto the window:

TO THE PEOPLE OF PARIS

In the grave circumstances now being experienced by Paris, the Prefecture of Police continues its mission.
It must preserve order and security in the capital.
We shall carry out this duty to the end.
Parisians, I count on you, as always, to facilitate my task.
Count on me.
Once more I assure you of my deep affection and total commitment.
Roger LANGERON

'To the end'. So this was it.

Clément hung up the phone as I stepped into the 'aquarium'. The room stank of feet, armpits and stale pipe smoke.

'For God's sake,' I said, 'couldn't you open a window?'

'They're painted shut, remember?'

He looked very pleased with himself, but also a little shifty, unwilling to meet my gaze. A file lay open on the desk before him. I recognised my own handwriting and realised it was the Fabricant file.

'Where did you get that?'

'The commissaire's desk,' he replied complacently. 'Someone's got to take this case on and make some progress.'

He smiled and ran a hand through his unruly hair as though weary after a particularly arduous yet satisfying shift – this from an officer who had taken the art of avoiding anything in the least onerous to unprecedented levels.

This was insufferable. I felt like punching him.

'What?' I said instead. 'What is it?'

'I've got your murderer, sweating it in the tank downstairs. Your "running man" walked in while you and the boss were out, Christ knows where.' He gave me a sly sidelong glance, 'He's an israélite, by the way.'

26

Realising that he was the 'running man' referred to in the affiches posted all over the arondissement, Yoav Lévy had put on his best black suit and Homburg hat and presented himself to the nearest police station.

And now he sat, blinking and swallowing hard, in the office of Commissaire Arthur Roland at the notorious Grande Maison, with the celebrated detective himself seated like a monument across the table from him. As usual, I maintained a palpable presence in the room, just out of the subject's sight.

Lévy was young – twenty, he said – but he looked even younger in his suit a size too large, like a boy dressed to impress a wealthy maiden aunt. He had bright black eyes like those of a bird and a wispy black beard, did Lévy, and he was hiding something from us.

'Why did you come forward now?' Roland asked, his gaze on the far corner of the ceiling where a cobweb fluttered gently in the faint draught rising from the river.

'I saw the notices – they asked me to.'

'Why were you running?'

'I was in a hurry.'

'Where were you going?' Roland's gaze dropped suddenly to fix on the disconcerted young man's eyes.

'Home.'

He had given an address in Rue du Prévôt, which Clément and Nevin, who had only just reappeared in the office, had been despatched to search.

'Why the hurry? Your home wasn't going anywhere without you.'

'I knew mother would have my dinner ready.'

'Where had you been?'

'To see someone.'

This was like listening to a reading from the Paris telephone directory one name at a time, from Aaberg to Zywicki, but with the pertinent information, the numbers, withheld. I had started by liking this youth but now I felt like hurrying him along with a swift clump to the head.

Roland, however, just pressed on. 'Who?'

He hesitated for a beat. 'I'd rather not say.'

'Where?'

'Boulevard Richard Lenoir.' He sighed.

For all his attempted evasions, young Lévy seemed more comfortable with a direct truth.

'So you got onto the Métro at Bastille?'

'Yes.'

'That's one stop. Walking down to the platform, waiting for a train, trundling along, getting out of the station... You could have walked it more quickly.'

He hesitated for longer this time, his right knee jiggling beneath the desk.

'I like the Métro.'

'Which car were you in?'

'The rear one, nearest the exit.'

'No. You were in First Class.'

'I wasn't.'

'Why did you kill him, son?' Roland asked in the tone of a kindly uncle offering his favourite nephew a pastry.

Lévy shook his head repeatedly. 'No... I didn't... I've never done anything wrong, only...'

He was crying. I leaned over his shoulder to offer him a handkerchief.

'Th-thank you,' he said, looking up at me pleadingly, his bright eyes filled with tears.

'It's all right, son, it'll feel better when you get it off your chest. Let's start with how you killed him.'

I understood that Roland did not believe in the young man's guilt. He merely wished to bring the interrogation to a swift and humane conclusion.

A rapid knocking at the door heralded the return of Clément and Nevin. The door opened and Clément peered in.

'You'll want to see this, boss.'

Lévy let out a despairing cry and banged his head against the back of his chair. His fists clenched as he shot Clément a wild and desperate look. Roland frowned and lowered his gaze and, after a second or two, followed Clément from the room.

I moved to perch on the side of the desk so that Lévy could see me, but I fixed my own gaze on the sluggish river below and waited.

'What's happening to me? I haven't done anything,' he wailed suddenly. His voice trembled: 'What are they doing? What are they showing him? Please, no...'

On the river, a steam barge chugged along, heading downstream, its cargo concealed under tarpaulins. Where normally one would see only the bargee, his mate and, perhaps, his wife, the deck was filled with people, standing-room only, suitcases piled high on the roof of the cabin.

Deprived of the count's immediate access to privileged information, people continued to flee the city in anticipation of its destruction, street by street, house by house. I wondered what fares they had been willing to pay, and the bargee to extort.

'Oh, I think you know what they're showing him, Yoav,' I guessed, still following the slow progress of the barge, 'don't you?'

Roland returned to the room, Nevin and Clément in his wake. Clément smiled unpleasantly into the frightened eyes of the young man, and then at me. Roland eased his bulk carefully into his seat and rapped

119

on the desk with a closed fist. Lévy, visibly trembling, groaned as he turned to face his inquisitor.

'My colleagues tell me that your father is a cabinet-maker,' Roland said.

Eager to please, relieved to be on safe ground, the young man nodded.

'Yes, that's right.'

'Is he good?'

'I think so, yes. He's a real craftsman, our papa.'

'He has his own workshop, I suppose.'

Lévy blushed and hung his head a little. 'The rents are too high.'

'So he works at home, in a room in your family apartment? No shame in that – lots of people do so.'

Yoav Lévy touched his forehead and closed his eyes.

'There's only the one room,' he mumbled.

'Yes, that's what my inspectors said – just the one room. He's a good, hard worker, your papa, but he isn't a wealthy man, would that be fair to say?'

'Yes, that's fair. He is a good man, a good father, a good carpenter, but not wealthy, no.'

Roland brought his fist to rest on the spotless blotter before him. When he removed the hand, two perfect little diamonds lay on the blotter. He looked at Lévy and Lévy looked at him, as a snared rabbit looks at the poacher in the moment before the blow falls.

'Explain these,' said Roland.

27

Oppressed by the presence of no fewer than four detectives and cornered by his own inability or unwillingness to explain the gems found among his possessions, young Lévy became distraught.

'But I walked in,' he kept saying, sometimes sobbing, sometimes in a daze, as though he hoped soon to awake from this nightmare. 'Why would I do that? Why?'

'Because you think we're stupid,' Clément replied on one occasion.

The boy, white-faced and pleading looked up at him aghast, his mouth opening and closing but no words emerging. Roland called a halt to it then, instructing Nevin and Clément to return the youngster to the tank, and ensure that he was fed.

'Go and have a think,' he said to Lévy. 'We'll talk again when you've had the chance to consider your position. Think, mind,' he said, raising a reproving finger and bringing it to rest against his temple as the lad was hustled away. 'I will have answers.'

When they had gone, he sat back in his chair with a profound sigh.

'He doesn't seem the type, does he? And no match for our man.'

'Well, he can't explain the diamonds,' I said, 'and we know that Rospeau, for one, used our man as a courier for large amounts of money... other valuables too, perhaps.'

'Diamonds,' said Roland, 'diamonds... we read a book once, back at school.'

For some reason, this announcement took me by surprise.

'English it was, translated into French though – Les Grandes Espérances it was called.'

'Charles Dickens, yes, Great Expectations in the English,' I said. 'That's a wonderful book.'

'That's the man. Well, in this book there's a character who keeps going on about the importance of "portable property", see, as if he reckoned a man or a family might get hounded out of their home at any moment, have to leave with what they could carry in their pockets.'

'John Wemmick, yes.'

'Well, I remembered him during my trip to Germany – you recall, I told you about that – and I saw what they were doing to the Jews there. I thought, those poor people need portable property, all right. Then they could get out of here.'

He opened a drawer and removed two envelopes, one large and full, the other a small white one in which he carefully sealed the diamonds before replacing it in the drawer. He put the large brown envelope down on the blotter, where the diamonds had been.

'Only, you won't get out, will you, Jojo?'

I shook my head. 'No, my place is here.'

'I thought you'd say that. Look, Jojo, one of the first things our new "masters" will do is to remove Jews from all public offices, especially the police. And, believe me, that'll be the least of it.'

'But I'm an atheist, I have no faith; neither did my father, nor my mother, my sister, my brother... I never even had a Bar Mitzvah... for God's sake I'm not even circumcised...'

'Aren't you?' he said, surprised.

'My parents thought it a Bronze Age practice born of superstition, a cruel mutilation of an unconsenting infant—'

'Anyway, it cuts no ice with them. It's race insanity with them.'

'And I'm French. My family's been French for generations—'

'I know, I know; but a French israélite.'

I felt sick, enraged with him though I knew he held no prejudice against me or any other person.

'I'm not having it, boss,' I said. 'I'm staying.'

'I've spoken to Monsieur Langeron about your... problem,' he said imperturbably.

'It's nothing to do with him either – it's not me who has the problem here!'

He regarded me kindly, sadness in his brown, spaniel eyes.

'What a world, what a time,' he said.

He was holding something out to me, something he'd extracted from the envelope.

'Take it, please, Jojo. The Prefect of Police himself has issued it for you, and changed your personnel record to match. It may keep you safe.'

It was a new warrant card bearing my photograph and the name Joseph Saint-Simon: such a small change, such a gulf in perceptions. I took it, fingered it suspiciously.

'Who else in the department knows your background?' He was still fiddling with the envelope, rather nervously, I thought.

'It never comes up. They mostly think I'm just a stuck-up bourgeois intellectual, I think – a bit of a prat, if you like. Clément sometimes has a dig, but he probably thinks that anyone who knows anything about books and music and art must be a Jew.'

'Ha! Probably, the moron.'

His face clouded. He mopped his brow with a handkerchief. I had never known him to break into a sweat before.

'On its own, your ID might not be enough, Jojo. If they suspect anything, they go back two generations –

baptismal certificates, marriage certificates, parents, grandparents, so I made a call to Fourbier the forger, called in a favour...'

He laid out a set of artfully aged documents on the pristine blotter. Fourbier was undeniably a master of his craft.

'No! How could you?' I spluttered, feeling the heat rise in my face. 'A complete pedigree of the "Saint-Simon" family, is it? Unimpeachably Catholic, Aryan, just as Descoups and that barmy old count would have me? No, no; I'm not having it!'

I became aware that my arms were flailing, my hands performing absurd chopping motions in the air.

He raised his hands in a gesture of appeasement. 'All right, it's too much, I understand.'

He slid the offensive envelope, containing the no-doubt perfect forgeries he had commissioned from Fourbier, into the bottom drawer of his desk, locked it and placed the key in the drawer in which he kept his never-ending supply of pencils.

'There,' he said, looking me directly in the eye and meaning at least two things at once. 'On your way out, would you ask Nevin to go back to the Lévy parents, find out where they keep any savings or float for the business; whether there's a bank account?'

I stood, momentarily unsure whether to protest or thank him, but I slipped the new warrant card into my wallet.

28

A light rain was falling as the three of us – Clément, Nevin and myself – made the short walk to the Préfecture of Police, answering the summons issued earlier that day to the entire body of the Paris police force by Monsieur Roger Langeron, the prefect. Roland had left much earlier, at about five, citing a rendezvous with the prefect at some unspecified location ahead of the general assembly.

I was astonished to discover that a number of stalls in the flower market between the Préfecture and the river remained open, and were even doing some desultory trade. Throughout the city, shopkeepers had deserted their posts and fled, leaving endless, disconsolate queues of women at the doors of the remaining boucheries, boulangeries, épiceries and crémeries.

Food distribution had all but broken down, the enemy were beating at our gates, yet here was an old chap limping away from a flower stall in the drizzle with a fragrant bunch of white carnations for his beloved wife. On reflection, I admired his order of priorities.

The Louis-Lépine room at the Préfecture was already crowded: pale, strained faces, broken chatter, subdued greetings between old friends and colleagues long separated by the demands of duty. A palpable sense of horror loomed over all, as though clouds of pestilence high up among the rafters were about to rain their burden down upon us through the anaemic light issuing from the electric chandeliers.

Amidst the crowd I noticed Peres and Picard, the ill-assorted pair of gardiens de la paix who had come to bring me to Saint-Paul Métro. Out of an urgent desire for relief from the general despair, I went to greet them.

'Bad times, Monsieur Inspector,' said old Peres, sucking his moustache. 'Still, like always it's up to us to hold the line, and that we will. That right, mate?'

He nudged young Picard with an elbow, rousing him from his trance, his helpless absorption in the collective nightmare. Startled, suddenly wide-eyed, the youngster nodded vigorously while Peres concluded.

'He'll stand with me, the lad, won't you, and keep the peace for the people?'

He gave Picard's pale face a sly sidelong glance and winked at me as though to say, He'll be all right, the lad, I'll keep him right.

Strangely cheered, I returned to my colleagues to find that Commissaire Roland had joined them.

'Been to see the American ambassador, Monsieur Bullitt,' he whispered to me. 'He's staying in Paris to hold the Boches to account, make sure they know the eyes of the world are on them.'

The room – about the same size as that mecca of music and dance, La Salle En Haut – continued to fill with commissaires and inspectors, with furtive types from the special branch, with beat police and traffic cops, with men and women alike, until there was no room to move and we stood shoulder to shoulder, like skittles in a box.

There must have been more than a thousand of us in the room when the trim, balding figure of Roger Langeron, the prefect of police, stepped onto the dais, his gold wire-framed spectacles glinting in the pallid light of the chandeliers, and his ascetic, scholarly face etched with deep furrows of sorrow and determination. He laid the situation facing the city – hopeless – before us without mitigation or embellishment, and the whole room heard him out in a silence at once reverent and desperate.

He authorised young women, mothers with young children, and officers at most risk from the enemy – Alsaciens-Lorrains, espionage and counter-espionage operatives – to flee the city, though many cried out to demur, vowing to remain at their posts.

And then he delivered us from utter helplessness. We would stick to our duty, we would maintain order, prevent looting and discourage actions that might provoke retaliation or reprisals. We would protect the people of Paris, we would fight crime and we would preserve the morale and spirit of our city.

Peres had put it more succinctly, but Langeron was an orator. At the conclusion of his speech, we cheered him and stamped until the chandeliers rattled and the floor quaked, and we departed with cries of 'Vive la France.'

As we left, we were intercepted by Commissaire Six, who drew Roland and me aside. Clément gave us a sour glance and grabbed Nevin by the shoulder and hurried him on – to a favourite bar, no doubt.

'Yes, Xavier,' said Roland, 'what is it?'

'I'm leaving tonight,' said Six with a gesture that suggested he might be about to vanish in a puff of smoke and sulphur. 'Rue Mesnil is all yours – it makes no difference now.'

Roland nodded solemnly and shot me a sharp glance.

'How's your case going, anyway?' Six asked with not the slightest trace of interest in his voice.

Roland looked down at him through narrowed eyes.

'We'll get there,' he said.

29

Late as it was, Madame Maurer was waiting for me, launching herself from her open door like a tiny terrier determined to teach the butcher's boy an unforgettable lesson.

'Monsieur Joseph,' she said accusingly.

She always addressed me by my given name to let me know that I had not yet earned the respect that was my late father, the eminent doctor's due.

'You have a young visitor, a friend of Mademoiselle Soubry.'

Ammarah, apparently, qualified as a credible adult and deserved to be accorded the respect of being known by her surname.

'And,' she said with relish, 'this place is being watched.'

'Watched?'

I thought of all the residents – the dentist, the carpet wholesaler, the poor but respectable workers in the rabbit hutches under the roof.

'That seems unlikely.'

'Oh, yes. They think they're being clever – different ones at different times, standing in different places; but then the same ones come round again. I see through them.' She tapped her brow just above the eye, 'Nothing gets past me on this street.'

As a youth, I had had occasion to discover the truth of this, and in consequence feel the agonising force of my father's mild disapproval.

'Where are they now?' I said, immediately feeling ridiculous when I found myself to be whispering.

'Corner of Brise-Miche,' she said without hesitation. 'He's a barrel-chested chap like my old man was. He's got a bad eye like an uncle of mine had.'

She mimed the presence of an eye-patch and portrayed a face drawn into a lop-sided rictus by some terrible injury.

'I'll take a look from upstairs,' I said and kissed her on the forehead, 'and thank you, you treasure.'

She smiled as I set off, taking the steps two at a time. Halfway up the first flight I stopped and called down to her.

'The phone lines, are they working now?'

She disappeared from view and, in an instant, reappeared at the door and nodded. I went on up.

They were drinking martinis on the sofa in the salon, chatting and laughing, one of my family's photo albums on Ammarah's knees, Louis Armstrong on the phonograph.

'Darling!' said Ammarah with a smile fit to warm the warrior heart of old Agamemnon himself.

I recognised the girl beside her but I didn't have time for that right now. I switched the lights off and twitched back the edge of the blackout curtain.

Ammarah laughed in the darkness at my back. 'I knew he wouldn't like me showing off his cute little baby bum, but...'

The road outside was dark and peaceful. I watched for a while until, at last, a match flared at the corner of Rue Brise-Miche. A flash-bulb glimpse of a stocky form, a thick forearm, an uplit face, bearded, and it was gone. But it was enough. Madame Maurer was right, and I was certain that it was my apartment they were watching.

I put the lights on, poured myself a glass of red and collapsed onto the bergère across from Ammarah and her new friend.

129

'Mademoiselle Mulot, isn't it? What brings you here?'

The girl from Rospeau's bar, Thomas Fabricant's old flame.

'Louise is staying here for a while,' said Ammarah. 'She has quite a story for you.' She nodded to the window, now securely blacked out again: 'What was that about?'

'Nothing I can't handle.'

Looking at her now, out of context, I realised what it was that I had recognised in Louise Mulot when she was standing behind the bar.

In an act of extravagant lèse-majesté, Rospeau had kitted her out to resemble the girl in Manet's A Bar at the Folies-Bergères. Who would have thought that such a low-rent rogue had ever even heard of the painting?

'Tell him about it, Louise, darling,' Ammarah urged, seizing her hand. 'Take your time.'

Their mood had changed, as though a thunder cloud had passed across the face of the sun.

Instead of going straight home from La Salle En Haut after leaving us the previous evening, Louise had gone to the riverbank where she and Tommy liked to walk. There she had wandered, numb and locked in spiralling, mournful reverie, until she did not know what hour. But it was dark when she arrived at Rue Sainte Geneviève, where she shared a tiny apartment with an infant-school teacher from the same small town in Normandy.

In the mental fog through which she felt her way, she noticed nothing amiss at first but, when she stumbled on the broken tread on the stairs leading up to the fourth floor, she realised.

'It was completely dark, Inspector, the gas lights were all out, all of them.'

She went on, holding tight to the bannister rail, until she reached the fourth storey landing, the floor beneath her attic rooms. There, strong arms seized her from behind, blocking her mouth so that she could make no sound.

'I thought, he is going to rape me. In my head I called out to Tommy to come and save me.'

She could smell the man's sweat, the cheap wine and tobacco on his breath. There was a gruff voice in her ear, strongly accented, not French.

'Where is he? Where is he? Tell me where he is and you can go. Where is he, where?'

Then Tommy did come to her rescue.

She remembered how he had painstakingly taught her how to defend herself should she be assaulted in the dark streets and alleys around her places of work. She let herself go limp, as though she had fainted. Taken by surprise, her assailant shifted his grip and she was able to reach up to her head. She withdrew the barbarously long pin that held her hair in place and thrust it blindly behind her.

'I heard him cry out and his hands went to his face. I'm almost sure I stabbed him in the eye. It felt horrible.'

A man with an injured eye. Somehow they had tracked her down here.

But she was suddenly free. As her assailant reeled and cried out in horror and agony, she ran down to the street and away into the night, turning first this way then that through back streets until she hardly knew where she was.

Finding herself suddenly out in the open, the stately bulk of Notre Dame rising like a castle keep across the river, she hastened over the bridge, fearfully conscious of the clacking of her heels on the pavement, and took refuge in the shadows at the door of the cathedral, pressing herself into the heaped sandbags as though they might somehow absorb and guard her slender frame.

Here she caught her breath and took stock, praying silently to God and the Virgin Mary to show her the way. Her prayers were answered when she remembered something that Ammarah had once told her – how she rarely bothered to make breakfast at home, but took herself most mornings to a café on Rue du Renard for coffee and a tartine.

'And so I thought of you, Inspector, and knew that if I could find Ammarah I'd find you – and I should be safe.'

'She hid until the café was open and then she waited there for me,' said Ammarah. 'So brave, to sit and wait all alone.' Her golden fingers closed around the girl's pale hand. 'And then we came home and we've been really getting to know each other while we waited for you to come.'

I thought about the man watching and waiting in the street outside – some nerve, to spy on the apartment of an inspector in the Police Judiciaire; and on a rota too. There was organisation behind this, something beyond the capability of Rospeau and his like, something with a whiff of brazen impunity about it. I didn't like it.

'I've got to get you out of here,' I said to the girl, 'get you somewhere really safe. Tonight.'

'There's something I didn't tell you about Thomas,' she said in a small voice, frightened again.

Ammarah squeezed her hand and nodded to encourage her.

'I don't know if it's important...'

30

Madame Maurer was still awake – I had always taken her apparently unsleeping vigilance for granted – and, thrilled by my suspicion that my phone might be tapped, she went to her gleaming Italian dresser, reverently removed the chintz cover from her venerable upright set and allowed me to call the duty officer at 36, looking on with smiles and sighs of satisfaction. Clément answered immediately, as though he had been expecting a call.

'Quiet night?' I asked.

'As the grave,' he replied. 'What's up, Simon? Got something?'

He was not drunk but he had clearly been drinking; he sounded almost friendly, collegiate. So I told him what I wanted and, for once, he raised no objection to helping a colleague out. A brief discussion with Madame Maurer established that the sisterhood of concierges would see to the rest.

At just after one in the morning I led Louise through the concierge's tiny apartment – cheap linoleum, a narrow bed in a recess, a table and two chairs, a soft armchair, the arms worn but adorned with lacy antimacassars, the high sheen of that massive dresser; everything spotless – and out through the courtyard door.

A sliver of pale light showed across the yard beyond the toilets and the now redundant pump, and I guided her towards it with no need of torchlight. The door opened fully to swallow us up and we found ourselves welcomed into the mirror image of Madame Maurer's living room by a large, breathless old woman with painfully swollen ankles showing beneath her widow's black habit. Puffing and wheezing, she opened the door to the entrance hall and showed us to the street door, which opened onto rue des Juges Consuls, a narrow passage around the corner from my own building and, I knew, out of our watcher's sight. We waited in silence in the darkness, pressed close to the massive door and shielded by the doorjamb.

We did not have long to wait. Within minutes a dark Traction Avant backed into the narrow street from rue de la Verrerie and glided silently to a halt in front of us, Clément at the wheel. I bundled Louise into the back and leaned in to speak quietly to my colleague.

'Get her a room at the usual place, Hôtel Atlantique, five nights on the department's account – should be plenty.'

In the obscurity I saw his large, uncombed head incline in solemn agreement, and then he restarted the motor and drew away. Louise Mulot's pale face looked back at me, eyes wide, bewildered by the vicissitudes of the last two days.

I sensed rather than heard someone approaching fast. I raised the electric torch I was carrying in my left hand, feeling for the switch, and with the other hand drew my automatic. The beam of light caught him full in the face, momentarily dazzling him. He raised an arm in involuntary defence, but not before I had recognised him as the brute who had been seated at the bar of La Salle En Haut when we came looking for Louise.

'Stop there,' I shouted, letting him see the handgun. 'Stay where you are!'

But my voice echoed in an empty street. He had fled, his swift feet silent over the cobbled road. Rubber soles: he had come well-prepared for his furtive errand. My own shoes clattered like a troop of cavalry as I ran in pursuit and careered round the corner, the light of the torch dancing erratically and elusively ahead of me like a promise in a dream.

I came to the edge of that seemingly permanent monument to utopian modernism, the wasteland of the plateau Beaubourg, and stopped. He could be anywhere. I had lost him. But I knew where to ask after him.

A mass of black cloud sat astride Paris like an incubus, and a light breeze carried the acrid perfume of burning petroleum, so that the few early-risers in the streets held scarves or handkerchiefs over their mouths and noses. Few shops remained open and the streets were free of traffic. Even the weary flow of refugees had dried to a trickle. The fearful wait for the invader had given way to apathy and despair.

On the wall of the prefecture facing the now abandoned flower market, a new poster had been pasted slightly askew, as though the bill-poster had been eager to get away:

NOTICE
To Residents of Paris
Paris having been declared an OPEN CITY, the Military Governor urges
the population to abstain from all hostile acts and counts on it to
maintain the composure and dignity required by these circumstances.

The Governor General of Paris
DENTZ

A smutty drizzle began to fall and I quickened my step, determined to arrive at 36 before the commissaire, so that I might lie in wait for him, armed with news of last night's events and Louise Mulot's surprising revelation.

He was already waiting for me in the 'aquarium', sitting at Nevin's small tin desk while the young detective made him coffee on the little burner we kept, strictly against regulations, in the corner. Clément was not yet in.

Balanced on a chair barely adequate for Nevin's trim backside, the neat array of small objects on Nevin's confined desktop before him – a portable typewriter, pencils in a stone jar, a notebook – the commissaire resembled a bull in a kindergarten.

'I hear you had a visitor last night,' he said, accepting with impeccable daintiness the tiny cup proffered by Nevin.

Inwardly I sighed with exasperation, but I tried not to let my frustration show.

'You've spoken to Clément?'

'Last night. I had to cut him short on account of the phone being tapped,' he said, quite unruffled.

'Your phone is tapped? Who would...?'

'And watchers on rotation in the street. Loiterers tend to stand out in my quarter.'

I was amazed at the scale and audacity of this operation, whatever its purpose.

'What the hell are we dealing with here?'

He shrugged and swallowed the scalding coffee in one gulp: 'Come to my office and tell me what you've got.'

Roland sat in silence, occasionally nodding, while I gave a full account of the recent adventures of Louise Mulot, ending with my recognition of the man who had been watching my building. When I had finished he continued to sit there, brow knitted in concentration, rhythmically tapping his chin with a pencil he had taken absent-mindedly from his breast pocket.

'Both of us under surveillance, the attack on the girl; it has to be about the Fabricant investigation,' I said, finding the silence intolerable. 'That man being at Rospeau's club – it's too much of a coincidence... but would Rospeau and his cronies have the men and the expertise to run an operation like this? And why? We told him – Fabricant is dead.'

'Perhaps he didn't believe us. It's clear that he – or someone – either doesn't know their man is dead, or doesn't believe it.'

Having thrown this pebble into the pool, he sat back and watched for the ripples.

'But why watch us, the police? It makes no sense... unless... unless... maybe he thinks we've got his diamonds. He said Fabricant carried money for him, maybe he used him as a courier for other valuables too. Those diamonds would represent a lifetime's savings for any ordinary man.

'Maybe young Lévy did kill Fabricant and take them, and Rospeau's put two and two together and thinks we've got them now and we're keeping them for ourselves – you know, given the situation, maybe he thinks that we reckon we can get away with it and cash in, in all the turmoil. He's known plenty of corrupt cops in his time, after all.'

'That's a lot of maybes,' he said. 'A lifetime's savings? For sure. Cash in, given the Germans will be here tomorrow? Makes sense to me.'

I felt as though a trapdoor had opened beneath me, as though I was watching a bar of purest gold turn to rust before my eyes. He opened the drawer, extracted the envelope in which he had sealed the gems and tipped its contents onto the unmarked blotter.

'Let's have another word with young Lévy, shall we?' he said. 'Let's see what he has to say about life savings, portable property and all that, eh?'

I exhaled in noisy relief and he gave me a puzzled frown.

'Then we can go and pay the Crapaud a visit.' He glanced at his watch. 'I reckon he'll be at breakfast in about an hour.'

'There is one other thing,' I said before going downstairs to collect Lévy from the tank. 'The girl says our man was seeing a psychiatrist – she'd thought he might be seeing someone else, another woman, so she went through his pockets one day and found a letter about a missed appointment.'

'Why didn't she say anything before?'

'Shame, I think.'

'About searching her chap's pockets or about him seeing a shrink?'

I shrugged: 'I know the doctor – Christophe Lefèvre, he was a friend of my father's – shall I call him and arrange for him to see us?'

32

Yoav Lévy winced as I removed the handcuffs and gripped him by the shoulders to guide him into the chair facing Commissaire Roland. He sat chafing his wrists and hands to restore circulation, his side curls drooping miserably, his sombre gaze drawn compulsively to the gemstones on the blotter. Roland sat in enormous immobility while I prowled the room, moving in and out of the youth's line of sight, watching his face.

'Your mum's worried about you, son,' said Roland, scratching his head and willing the boy to engage with the fatherly concern in his mournful brown eyes. Lévy looked up at him and seemed about to say something, but Roland raised a restraining hand. 'I popped in to see her, your mum, on my way here this morning; your dad, he was there too, worried sick. They want you home, lad.'

As Lévy began to weep, his nose ran with snot and he looked suddenly like a small, frightened child. Roland took an enormous white handkerchief from his pocket and, leaning across, folded the boy's hand around it.

'I, I, I...' Lévy stuttered.

'Time to tell us the truth, son. Come on, Yoav, your mum and dad and me, we chatted a while and we're almost there. We know, you see, but I need to hear it from you. Never mind about the small stuff, no one's going to worry about that right now, just take your time and tell us, eh?'

'I never hurt anyone,' Lévy managed to say at last, 'I don't think I ever could.'

'I know, son, but you did do something, didn't you, something that made you afraid to tell us the truth?'

Yoav nodded, took a little time to dry his nose and eyes and compose himself then, haltingly at first, made his confession.

He had read a lot about the Nazi regime, had Yoav, between the lines and all, and he had spoken to new neighbours who were recent refugees from Germany; and everything he read and heard terrified him. For weeks, months, he had been battering in vain at the ramparts of his parents' complacency – 'Not in France, my love, not in Paris, it's unthinkable' – until finally he had felt compelled to act.

'Jewish bank accounts aren't safe under those people,' he said, 'and Jewish homes are raided, destroyed, everything stolen.'

So he went to the bank, where everyone knew him for his father's son, where he had many times made deposits, and sometimes withdrawals, for his father. And he presented a cheque made out to cash. Not for everything, measuring his actions carefully to avoid suspicion, but for most; his father's life savings.

'How did you get your father to sign the cheque?' I asked.

He smiled for the first time, rather sweetly resembling a mischievous child. 'It wasn't the first time I'd copied his signature. Sometimes I used to feel like a day off school.'

I went to whisper in Roland's ear, 'Would you like me to check with the bank?'

'No point, they're all shut, managers scarpered,' he said aloud. 'I reckon you got there just in time, lad, eh?'

After the bank he went to the vase in which his mother kept the cash she saved against the unforeseen and he took most of that too.

'I knew – I'd heard about – a man, I can't say who, who could help.'

141

'A man who deals illegally in diamonds,' Roland stated. 'You're going to have to tell us his name, son.'

Yoav shook his head and gripped the edge of the desk. 'I can't. We're going to be in enough trouble with the Germans. I'm not going to have him after my family as well.'

His face was set, determined, and he suddenly looked a grown man.

'You know what?' said Roland. 'If your dealer is the man I think he is, you're lucky he didn't take your money and kick you out into the street. Instead of which, it looks as though he dealt with you fairly. Surprising, really, but people do surprise even me sometimes. Perhaps I'll let it go this time.'

'You were within easy walking distance of home,' I said from behind Lévy, into his left ear. 'Why take the Métro, why run from the station?'

He turned his head to face me, his expression open and earnest: 'I was carrying everything my family has in the world, Inspector. I needed to be safely home as quickly as I could – I was terrified someone would rob me, so I moved fast and in public, both ways.'

'But you only drew attention to yourself,' I said. 'As Monsieur the Commissaire says, you were very lucky – on another day you would have been robbed.'

'I see that now,' he said, thoroughly deflated and slumped in his seat. 'And I've lost the diamonds anyway.'

The diamonds sat on the blotter, glinting gaily, mockingly. He could reach out a hand and scoop them up but, as contraband in the possession of the State, they were forever irrecoverable. Lévy began to weep again.

'All right,' said the commissaire softly, 'you're in the clear. You can go.'

Roland shovelled the diamonds into his great hand and tipped them back into the envelope, all the while searching my face for signs of emotion. Still looking at me, he slid the envelope across the desk to Lévy.

'And don't forget these,' he said.

I almost laughed aloud from relief.

'We'd better make sure you get home safely,' he said. 'Get an officer to escort Monsieur Lévy home, would you,' he said to me. 'Nevin, not Clément, I think.'

As I led the stunned young man from his office, Roland picked up the telephone and asked for the strongroom, where evidentiary exhibits were stored.

33

Every Thursday morning, beneath the canopy of its linear forest of plane trees, Boulevard Richard-Lenoir played host to one of Paris's busiest and most raucous markets, laying the sumptuous produce of regional farms and market gardens before the populace of the city.

Every week without fail, stalls and barrows and upturned boxes would line up to create a narrow lane in the centre of the broad avenue, many stacked with seasonal fruits and vegetables, and salads of every hue and variety. Above other stalls skinned rabbits would hang by their feet like the victims of some byzantine torture alongside corpulent hams, blushing like brides. And then there would be the plucked carcasses and hewn portions of poultry, and jars of home-prepared confit duck and foie gras, and fat country snails, nestling together in their liquor like an indecent suggestion. And unctuous slabs of butter would be sweating under muslin, and fifty or sixty varieties of cheese would send forth their odoriferous invitation from one side of the lane to the other; and gleaming fish would lie on marble slabs with eels still wriggling on trays beside them; and red-faced butchers, grown plump on their own wares, would strenuously strive to outshout each other (and provoke thoroughly profane laughter in the head-scarved crowds of browsing women and each other) in proclaiming the superior length, girth, firmness and flavour of their sausages.

Today, however, there was nothing but a couple of miserable barrows bearing sacks of new potatoes and forlorn bundles of wilting greens, and a bent old woman in black, apparently unperturbed by the persistent drizzle as she oscillated between the stalls in a resolute quest to determine which of them offered best value for her widow's two mites.

Clément had eventually come to light, having emerged, yawning and stretching, from the vacated office of an inspector who had returned to his old artillery regiment as soon as war was declared. Roland had frowned in displeasure and, to teach him a lesson, promptly appointed him our driver for the morning.

With no more than a passing glance, full of passionate yearning, at the coffee pot in the aquarium, Clément had snapped to it with astounding eagerness and taken himself directly to the garage to find a suitable vehicle. If I had witnessed my mother's indolent and ill-tempered cat playing fetch with all the avid attentiveness of a Labrador retriever, I could not have been more astonished.

Now the commissaire commanded Clément to pull over, and the Peugeot eased to a halt in front of a dingy café with blacked-out windows on which a copy of the Governor General's ominous notice had been posted in the night. The door was guarded by a sizeable brute wearing a frayed suit in a nauseating shade somewhere between rust and ochre, and a flat cap pulled low over the eyes.

Roland instructed Clément to wait, descended from the car and led me to the door of the café. The doorman squinted at us suspiciously and extended a strong arm to obstruct us. He had a broad, weather-beaten face, horribly torn and deformed ears, and a flattened nose like that of an unsuccessful boxer.

'Would you like me to break that for you?' Roland inquired conversationally, nodding at the obstructive arm.

The man peered into Roland's face as though he was short-sighted and struggling to make out the features.

'Le Bourreau!' he exclaimed at last. 'I ain't seen you in years.'

'It's a wonder you can see anything with those peepers, Pépé. You want to get yourself a pair of specs.'

'You know me, Arti, too vain.'

'Ha! Is he in?'

'Is who in?'

Normal professional discourse seemed to have resumed.

'Don't bother with all that,' said Roland. 'Look at my poor young inspector, he's getting soaked out here. He'll catch his death.'

Pépé did indeed give me a good look up and down, and seemed unimpressed with what he saw.

'Ain't they feeding you coppers, no more?'

'The Crapaud, pal, is he in? He'll be expecting us, sooner or later.'

At that moment the door opened and a bare-footed young woman with tousled bleached hair, still in her dressing-gown, said, 'It's OK, stand down, soldier, he'll see them.'

Pépé seized Roland's hand and shook it warmly. 'You must come for a drink with us, Arti, the old crowd, the team. We're always talking about you, remembering...'

Roland smiled and extracted his hand.

'Someday, Pépé, someday.' And, I thought to console his old comrade with the knowledge that he, too, was remembered, he told me, 'Pépé was a prop forward with me in the old days – strength of an ox.'

146

'That's right,' said the doorman to our backs as we entered the dark and deserted café, 'the old days. Silver medals in the Olympic Games we had – twice.'

The café seemed a decent enough place if a little dark and run down, and I could readily imagine popping in for a coffee and a light lunch if I were manning a stall on the market or, rather more likely, shopping with Ammarah. The young woman in the dressing gown had retreated behind the counter, where she was drying glasses, and I gave her an appraising glance in passing: not bad.

Rospeau, who was today wearing a dark suit and a bright yellow waistcoat, was seated in a curtained booth at the back of the café, a large plate of pastries, a jug of coffee and a bottle of Marc on the guéridon before him. The appetising aromas of freshly-brewed coffee, warm croissants and apricot jam suffused the cubicle and I realised that my mouth was watering like the maw of a ravenous hound.

In order to arrive at work as early as possible, I had skipped the breakfast of stale bread and biscuits on offer at home and now I felt suddenly, agonisingly hungry. Where in today's Paris, I wondered, had Rospeau managed to obtain such delights? With difficulty, I refrained from asking.

'Have a seat, Commissaire... Inspector,' said Rospeau genially, 'will you join me in a little morning freshener?'

He nodded towards the bottle of Marc.

'It's good stuff – from my brother's place, down south. My wife and kids are down there now,' he added nostalgically.

The girl came over and placed two clean glasses on the table. I could smell the sleep still on her.

'For Christ's sake, get dressed,' Rospeau said, but his gaze lingered on the opening of her dressing gown as she

147

leaned over to deliver the glasses, and he could not suppress the smile that touched his lips.

'Not for us,' said Roland, not feeling the need to consult me.

'A pastry then, some apricot preserve perhaps? It's the best, the one they serve the king of England – I have it sent over from Fortnum and Mason,' the English names strangled at birth on his southern tongue.

He made an open-handed gesture to emphasise the munificence of his hospitality. Without thought or hesitation I reached over, took a croissant and began to wolf it down. Rospeau smiled triumphantly and sat back with his warty hands entwined on his canary chest.

'What can I do for you gentlemen today?'

Roland came straight to the point: 'When we came to your club to speak to Mademoiselle Mulot there was a man at the bar.'

'Was there? I don't recall.'

There was an unctuous core of apricot jam at the centre of the croissant. Furtively, I licked my fingers.

'Try. He was the only customer.'

He pursed his lips and looked towards the tar-browned ceiling in a pantomime of remembrance. Finally he shook his head and took a sip of coffee. As he dipped his head, birdlike, to drink I saw that his slicked-back hair concealed an extensive area of baldness.

'No, sorry.'

'Do we really have to go through this routine again?' Roland said wearily. 'Perhaps your memory will improve after we've been over this place and your apartment upstairs and confiscated your stash of black market diamonds.'

Rospeau was startled.

'Apartment?' was all he could manage.

'That's right, Claude, your nice big apartment on the first floor, just through that door behind you and up the stairs. Or perhaps you have an elevator?'

He surrendered.

'He's a chum of Tommy's, one of his ex-Foreign Legion lot, works the door sometimes, occasionally comes in for a drink and to eye up the girls when he's not working.'

'Works for you then.'

'For Tommy. They all work... worked for Tommy. I pay Tommy, he pays... paid them, that's how it worked. To be honest, I was surprised to see him there that day. Most of the ex-Foreign Legion lads have cleared off out of Paris – don't fancy their chances when the Chleuhs come.'

'Name?'

'They call him Niki, don't know his surname but he's Russian, I think.'

'Where would we find him?'

Rospeau shrugged theatrically. 'He never handles my money, so I don't know or care where he goes. Bars, cafés, fleapit hotels, the usual...'

'Your hotel? The one beneath the club?'

He shrugged again. 'Who knows? We get all sorts – as long as they pay...'

'It seems he doesn't know Tommy's dead, and is out looking for him. Why would that be?'

'Owes him money, perhaps? How would I know?'

'All right. Did you give him, or anyone else, Louise Mulot's address?'

Behind us the bell jingled, indicating that a customer had managed to get past Pépé and enter the café. Rospeau poured himself a large measure of Marc and pointed to the two spare glasses with an eyebrow raised in inquiry. Roland shook his head.

'Well?'

'Look, I don't even know her address, right? Barmaids and hat check girls come and go, they're just not important. I don't go round collecting their addresses, all right?'

He was flustered, irritated. I guessed that the customer who had just arrived was of some importance to him, and he wished us gone.

Roland sighed and settled more heavily into his seat. He selected a dainty cinnamon pastry from the plate and consumed it with incredible slowness.

'You know what?' he said at last, wiping his mouth with the back of his hand, 'I think I'm about to choose to believe you, Claude, but first you need to tell me about this Niki's politics. How's that for a deal?'

'Sure, why not? They all did bits and pieces for that crackpot count, you know, the Chevaliers of something or other.'

'The ones you said you'd never heard of...'

'Yeah, well, Tommy worked for him, they all did – he liked to think he had his own private army, and he paid well apparently. Twat!'

So the count and his Chevaliers had the personnel to run a round-the-clock surveillance operation and it seemed that, for reasons unknown, they either disbelieved us when we informed them that Fabricant was dead, or felt some compelling need to verify the fact. Roland nodded as though he had known already.

'One last thing,' he said.

Rospeau looked apprehensive.

'Looks like you gave that young Israélite, Lévy, a fair deal – credit to you for that. You going soft, Claude?'

'Lévy, was that his name? Well, he paid a fair price... Besides, he was a good kid, looking out for his mum and dad...'

Rospeau smiled, showing his pointed teeth; the smile of a caiman. With a sinking feeling in my stomach I

150

realised that the gems he had sold to young Lévy were as likely as not to be fakes, worthless paste.

As we drew aside the curtain to leave, I glanced around to locate Rospeau's new visitor. A young woman sat at a table near the counter, stirring a cup of coffee, her face averted from us. In the half-light it was impossible to be sure, but I thought I knew her from somewhere. It was only when we had settled into the car after a dash through the now established rain that I remembered.

It was Madame Lederer, one of our witnesses from the crime scene, no doubt come to purchase her own piece of portable property.

34

Like my late father, Dr Christophe Lefèvre saw his private patients in his own home, a large first floor apartment above a shop specialising in all kinds of optical equipment on the short stretch of Rue de Rivoli between the Hôtel de Ville and the Tour Saint-Jacques.

Clément drew the Peugeot smoothly to a halt in front of the store and, since we were now within easy walking distance of 36, Roland sent him off with the car as soon as we had alighted.

Idly, I browsed the shop window while the commissaire gave Clément his instructions. Here was every manner of device for looking at things, looking into things, looking out at things, the better to see. I wondered what apprehensions such a display must provoke in people about to visit a psychiatrist for the first time.

We passed the concierge with a flash of our IDs and arrived punctually for our appointment at noon. The doctor himself opened the door to us.

'Uncle Christophe' was a fat and rather joyous man, quite unlike anyone's idea of an alienist, and he greeted me with an enormous enveloping hug, the bristles of his full grey beard tickling my cheek.

'My little Joseph,' he cried, laughing aloud from pleasure at seeing me after all this time. 'How wonderful – a full-grown detective.'

I had not seen him since my father's funeral the previous year, and then he had held both me and my brother in his arms as we tried to hold back the tears. Rachel, away across the ocean, had been unable to make it home in time.

'Your father was so proud of you,' he said, 'so pleased you'd found your own way, and so proud.'

I hadn't known that and was uncertain of its absolute veracity, but his sincerity, like so much about him, was so warm and transparent that I felt comforted anyway.

'Your mother is well?'

'She's safe in Quebec, staying with Rachel and her husband.'

'And Paul?'

I shrugged and shook my head, my stomach churning as it always did when I thought of the perils my brother faced.

'He's with the army.'

He nodded, his plump, ruddy face radiating concern. 'We must continue to hope.'

'And the great Commissaire Roland, France's foremost detective, too,' he cried, grasping the commissaire's enormous hand in two of his own. In a lower tone, 'I can't tell you how much it meant to us when you stood on our platform and spoke out against the death penalty, Commissaire; no indeed.'

I stared at Roland in surprise and with yet greater regard.

'After the despicable show at the Weidmann execution, who could honourably support it any longer?' the commissaire replied.

Roland had been instrumental in bringing Eugen Weidmann's killing spree to an end and, as one of the arresting officers, was expected to witness his public execution. The conduct of the crowd at the execution was so egregiously foul that the practice of public execution was immediately halted.

'If justice must be dealt in secret, for fear of people behaving like wild beasts, then it's no sort of justice at all,' Roland said, shaking his head in dismay at humanity.

Dr Lefèvre reluctantly relinquished the commissaire's hand to show us the way to his study, which overlooked the quiet courtyard at the back of the apartment. The room was large and light despite the grim black clouds overhead, and evidently doubled as his consulting-room.

Above a roll-top desk was a monochrome print in which a roaring minotaur lunged at a young girl who carried nothing but a candle and a posy. Between these archetypal figures a half-naked woman was slumped over her panicked horse, apparently passed out or dead already.

'You like that? It's by Pablo Picasso,' said my father's old friend, observing me looking. 'Only a print, I'm afraid. Do you know him? No? Perhaps your dad did. Hmm, I think so. Interesting chap, very interesting...'

For a moment I was uncertain whether it was my father or this artist whom he found interesting.

The rest of the wall-space was taken up by bookshelves crammed with volumes dealing with internal medicine, ancient history, human anatomy, psychology and psychoanalysis, English, French and German grammar, anthropology, carpentry, mathematics and comparative theology; as well as novels and collections of poetry in at least four languages. Uncle Christophe was a byword in my family for a polymath.

'Ah,' he said self-deprecatingly, 'I see my disgracefully disorganised little library catches your attention – the great unread for the most part I'm afraid, eh? Borrow as you choose, dear boy.'

A modern straight-backed chair was placed between the desk and a black leather couch, and four well-stuffed armchairs surrounded a low table on which was a silver tray bearing bone china cups with a dragon motif, a steaming pot of coffee and a jug of hot milk.

Observing my sceptical glance at the couch, Dr Lefèvre laughed.

'You're wondering about the couch, Joseph? Sometimes I like a little nap in the afternoon – not getting any younger, eh? So now you know my little secret,' he tapped his nose conspiratorially, 'but I find it unsuited to clinical purposes, huh?

'A doctor and his patient should be able to look each other in the eye, don't you think? Between ourselves, I hear that the story behind the use of the couch in psychoanalysis is that Dr Freud had a phobia of being stared at, so he took to sitting out of sight, behind his patients. Wouldn't suit me in the least. No, not at all. Not your dear father either, I believe.'

'Please,' he said, indicating that we should sit.

As he poured, he looked at each of us in turn: 'I was extremely sad to hear of the violent death of my patient, and of course I would like to offer any help within my power. What would you like to know? The poor man is dead now, and the dead are permitted few secrets.'

I thought of my father's all-consuming interest in archeology, the bringing to light of the subterranean secrets of the long dead. Archeology, psychiatry, detective work – all seeking to discover the hidden history behind the presented fact. Commissaire Roland was right about that.

'What would you like to tell us, doctor?' Roland replied.

'You know him as Thomas Fabricant, the name he assumed after leaving the Legion, where his nom de guerre had been Thomas Vaillant; but the name his mother knew him by, the name he kept so well-guarded, was Tomáš Weil.'

A sweep of the arm described the safe confines of the bright, cosy room he had created.

'Here, you see, only the naked truth is of any use, and I think he came to see that. Tomáš Weil was who he was.'

Captain Thomas Vaillant had been referred to Dr Lefèvre by the chief medical officer attached to the Foreign Legion following his honourable discharge with full French citizenship in 1937, after five years service.

'There were things he couldn't get out of his mind,' Dr Lefèvre explained, 'even in his sleep these experiences tormented him in the form of recurring nightmares. And he was jumpy, irritable, too quick to anger; and then at times he would find human contact intolerable and would have to lock himself away, sometimes literally and sometimes by withdrawing mentally and emotionally, an extreme form of detachment.

'He regretted very much the effect that his disturbance must be having on his girlfriend, among others. But he found, I think, a kind of refuge in the company of fellow veterans, men who had shared at least a portion of his experience.'

I looked up from the notebook in which I had been scribbling. Roland was nodding slowly, but with a puzzled frown.

'Very often, you understand,' the psychiatrist said, 'it is the wrongs that we do that cause us far more pain than the wrongs done to us, and this was the case with Tomáš. In the course of his duties, he did such things for France... things beyond the scope of the average man's worst nightmares.'

In the Legion, he had quickly been identified as an individual of exceptional intelligence, linguistic ability, physical strength and endurance; and, above all, he possessed an abundance of those qualities of controlled rage and existential despair that make a veritable Achilles of a soldier. So Tomáš was selected for special duties, intensively trained and schooled, and set upon the enemy.

'You see, across Morocco and Algeria there is the ever-present, simmering grievance of a people denied.'

'The Berbers,' I said, thinking suddenly of the old woman in the zone, and more particularly of her absent son.

'The Berbers,' the doctor agreed. 'Grievances unaddressed do not wither away. In fact, given leadership, they often grow into armed revolt. The mission that Tomáš was given – alone and deniable – was to move undercover among the Berber population, usually in the guise of an itinerant salesman dealing in fabrics, that sort of thing, but with a nice little sideline in firearms. His task was to identify effective leaders and make them silently disappear, to prevent a recurrence of the earlier troubles in the region, you understand.'

'Kill them?' said Roland.

'Kill them, yes, but sometimes, if the circumstances were propitious, he would do more than kill them, he would make them vanish, make it look as though they had deserted the cause, or had perhaps been informers, sowing unease and distrust throughout the organisation. His victims were many, men and women alike.

'It would have required immense courage, calmness in the face of constant pressure, both external and internal, and a considerable degree of ruthlessness, the dissociation of all human tenderness. This was no easy matter because Tomàš, you understand, is far from the sort of man one might regard as a natural killer – by no means psychopathic or morally insane, whichever term you prefer – but an essentially normal individual.'

'The dangers he must have faced...' I interjected, thinking involuntarily of my little brother.

'Yes, he spoke often of the effects of living in a state of constant fear of discovery, exposure, and what would follow. And then the terrible things he did, worse even than the bloody deeds men are normally required to commit in times of war – I doubt I ever heard the worst of it, because–'

'He stopped coming,' Roland interrupted him. 'You had to send him a letter – addressed, of course, to Thomas Fabricant – to try to prompt him to return and finish his work with you.'

'Indeed, but he didn't come back. I last saw him some three months ago, and heard no more from him.'

'After, what, two years of regular sessions?'

'About that, yes. I could check the precise date...'

Roland raised a hand to indicate that this would not be necessary.

'What about his early life, his origins?'

'He was born in Prague, the only child of a Jewish father and a Catholic mother, who ran a moderately successful restaurant. Other than insisting on his circumcision for reasons of family tradition, his father was not a religious man and Tomáš was brought up in the Catholic faith, to which he still ardently adhered. Tomáš did exceptionally well at school and went to the university in Prague to study medicine.

'There he met a girl, his first cousin on the paternal side, who was studying at the university. They fell in love and would have married but for the violent opposition of her large family – "business" people in a country town, I forget where.

'Now, her family – her father and her brothers – were a pretty... well, shall we say rugged set of individuals involved in a wide range of criminal activity alongside their legitimate interests – smuggling, extortion, kidnapping, currency fraud – and they were used to getting their own way, by lethal force if necessary. In fear of his life, Tomáš fled the country, leaving his beloved in the hands of her family.'

158

'The shame,' said Roland.

'You have it, Commissaire, the shame, the bitter, lingering aftertaste of what he saw as his cowardice – regret, remorse, shame, bottomless self-loathing...'

'Poor lad.'

'And as to what happened to his lover, he never knew. He never heard word of her again.'

'Did he fear that they might still be looking for him, even here?' I asked.

'We discussed it. It was always a possibility – they are vengeful folk, by his account, highly mindful of their prestige, their so-called honour, but he never picked up any hint or sense of their presence here and, remember, he was trained and extremely adept at detecting surveillance or undue interest – too long a look from a stranger in a bar or a gaze too quickly averted, the beautiful but overly flirtatious woman suddenly at his elbow, the same man encountered twice in one day... He wouldn't have survived so long undercover otherwise.'

'Everyone slips up eventually,' said Roland. 'One thing puzzles me though, doctor.'

The doctor nodded, scratched his beard: 'I think I can guess...'

'Why would a man who's broken down because of the murder and mayhem he's been committing in the army want to get involved in violence again – running the door at clubs, working for mobsters and fascists?'

'Now, that is a very good question, Commissaire. We humans do seem to possess a most regrettable compulsion to repeat, to revisit our traumas – are France and Germany not at war again? I was working on that with him, but I'm afraid I have no compelling solution to offer.'

As we were about to leave he detained us a moment at the door.

'I heard an excellent joke in a café the other day, very pointed, very apt,' he said. 'It went like this: why are so many roads in France lined with trees?'

Observing with satisfaction our baffled expressions, he provided the answer.

'Because the Germans like to march in the shade!'

His feverish laughter followed us down the stairs.

35

The rain had stopped and we strolled through eerily empty streets to the restaurant on Place Dauphine for lunch. Everywhere shops were shut and secured behind steel or wooden shutters. The throaty roar and rumble of Paris traffic had given way to a frozen silence broken only by the distant gunfire and the symphonic song of a blackbird, still commanding his little kingdom from the top of an aspen tree on the riverbank. Around him, the leaves shook and shivered in the light breeze as though in fear of all that was to come.

But no street musicians played, no children skipped and laughed in delight at the unexpected freedom afforded them by the closure of their schools, no angler shouted boasts to his mates about the size of yesterday's catch, and no lover whispered honeyed, voluptuous words in the blushing ear of his beloved. Even the bouquinistes' green boxes were firmly shut, feebly padlocked against the coming of the barbarians.

The restaurant was closed. On the shuttered window a damp affiche offered scant reassurance that it would ever re-open. In sorrow and self-pity we made our way to the préfecture and its notorious clubhouse, which had been managed until recently by an unabashed fugitive from justice going by the name of Henri Normand. The brief, invigorating reign of Normand, or to give him his birth name, Chamberlin, breathed pure oxygen into the still, dead waters of the place and brought it to such life that I once heard someone laugh there. Even the food improved.

But life is anarchy, time breaks rocks and hierarchies, and geology and standing orders must always have the last laugh. Normand permitted himself too generous a margin, was inevitably caught and consigned to the infallible mill of justice, and normality settled upon the clubhouse like a shroud. The sanctimonious sigh of satisfaction seemed audible still, the moment one set foot there.

Liberated from the profiteering presence of Chamberlin, the clubhouse could offer only an unprepossessing plate of pale, flaccid sausage served with pickled cabbage and – a regrettable innovation – noodles swimming in a sauce with the colour and consistency of pond water. Roland ate with dogged unconcern, finishing the lot in minutes, while I quailed in revulsion and nibbled on a hunk of bread. Surreptitiously watching him, I suddenly remembered the evening when he had invited me to dine at his home.

Héloïse Roland had accepted with expressions of delight the wilting posy I had brought from the flower market, and immediately steered me to the kitchen where, as she trimmed the stems of the blooms, she identified each by name before setting them in a porcelain vase. I watched her, fascinated. She can only have been a handful of years younger than her husband but she had about her a lightness of being, a figure and a profile more than merely redolent of the beautiful young school-teacher who must have captivated the celebrated athlete and newly-fledged police officer of some decades past.

At table, her conversation was bright and wide-ranging, her understanding acute. She successfully refereed a brief skirmish in the matter of homework between her husband and daughter (then a lycéenne, now a law student) and even persuaded the shy young girl to give it a turn on the piano. By the end of the evening I was pretty much ready to fall in love with her myself.

She cooked us a simple but exquisite meal of poulet à la crème de l'estragon and tarte aux pommes bracketed by courses of soup and cheese, and Roland knocked each plate back in heedless moments. From across the table, his wife appealed to me in comic despair.

'Really, Arthur,' she had laughed. 'If I fed you the cat's boiled fish, I swear you wouldn't notice.'

I had loved the sound of her laughter, unforced, like that of a child at play.

'Right,' said the commissaire, mopping his plate with another sop of bread and dabbing delicately at his lips with the coarse canteen napkin, 'let's summarise.' He looked at me expectantly.

'Sunday evening, dead man found on Métro, Line 1,' I said. 'Found by Monsieur Julien De Nouailles – who we now know is close to the leadership of the Chevaliers de la France Catholique – and his mistress. Her cries attract the doctor and nurse from the next carriage, and the refugee couple who'd just got off on their way to a new home and jobs, stop to see what's going on. Young Lévy testifies that, from the platform of Bastille, he saw only one person in First Class, a man, apparently sleeping, so he was probably dead by then. Fabricant got on at Reuilly-Diderot...'

'Hold on. How do we know that?'

I thought again: 'Well, he bought a carnet of tickets at a café-tabac virtually next to the station, but I take your point. All right, Reuilly-Diderot is the latest he could have got on because he was dead by Bastille and his killer wasn't in the carriage then, so must have got off at Gare de Lyon by the latest.'

'Right, so it seems more likely that he and his killer, possibly but not necessarily together, got on before Reuilly-Diderot – at Nation or Porte de Vincennes. That allows more time to – what? – strike the lethal blow, remove his ID, throw the acid...'

'It wouldn't take long – seconds in the hands of a professional, easily accomplished between stops. Reuilly-Diderot is still a strong possibility.'

Roland nodded slowly.

'We got a firm identification of the man who bought the tickets from the woman at the tabac, as well as a lead to where we might find out more about him. Our man was working for a known figure in organised crime in Rospeau, and for a new bunch of fascists in the count's mob. That feels more and more significant to me – it just feels it. Our man was working as some kind of mercenary – or, just as likely, a fanatical activist – for fascists at the very moment that the Nazis are about to take over the city.

'God knows what contacts the count's people have already had with them – what part they expect to play in a German occupation. I imagine that's why a man of the count's standing is still to be found in Paris – looking to open, or continue, negotiations. And what did our man know about it? Perhaps that's why he was silenced... Or perhaps he played a more prominent role in it than we've so far considered...'

Roland raised his hand. 'We've just learned that our man had a Jewish father. Why would he collaborate with Nazis?'

'He was a Catholic. He was chased out of his own country, out of his career, and away from the woman he loved by Jews.'

He nodded slowly again, stroking his chin: 'All right.'

'And now Dr Lefèvre tells us that his patient had been a one-man programme of state-organised assassination in the Maghreb, knocking off the potential leadership of a renewed Berber revolt. I'd say we have two groups firmly in the frame with strong revenge motives and, most likely, with the required expertise –

Berber radicals and the Jewish gangsters from back home.

'Not to mention rival far-right factions, the communists, and the usual suspects in organised crime in Paris – Rospeau's rivals or Rospeau himself if Fabricant had had his fingers in the till. When you think about it, just about everyone in Paris had a motive to do away with him. All in all, it's a wonder he survived so long.'

Roland gave a gale force sigh.

'We need to go back to the start. I've asked Nevin to bring that young doctor – Caron? – to my office this afternoon.' He inspected his watch. 'He should be waiting there now. Let's hear his story again.'

36

Dr Caron sat on a wooden chair outside Roland's office, Hugo's Le Dernier Jour d'un Condamné open in his hands. He was clearly too nervous to read though, his eyes constantly scanning the unfamiliar surroundings like a young deer on the alert for wolves. I noticed that he was wearing the same brown suit and scuffed boots – medical interns, even the best ones, didn't get paid much it appeared. As he watched us approaching from the stairwell, he ran his fingers through his thick fair hair and moistened dry lips with the tip of his tongue.

'Good afternoon, doctor,' said Roland with a smile. 'Thank you so much for coming in to see us.' He noticed the book in the young man's hands and sought to put him at his ease. 'Hugo, eh? I must get around to reading him one day – any good?'

Rather awkwardly, Caron stood and offered a hand to be shaken, his face as pale and drawn as that of a condemned man, as though he expected that we might slap handcuffs on the proffered wrist and set him on the path to the guillotine. Roland shook his hand, opened the office door and stood aside to allow him to enter. I followed and stood at the door while they arranged themselves on either side of the desk.

'Right,' said Roland opening the file that Nevin had delivered to his desk, 'You were in car four, immediately behind First Class, is that right?'

'Yes,' croaked Caron, closing his eyes the better to visualise the scene. Or, I thought, in despair at being obliged to confess his immediate proximity to the murdered man.

'The train pulled into Saint-Paul... then what?'

'We...'

'With respect, doctor, you're the only one sitting here. Speak only for yourself.'

'I heard a scream, a woman sobbing, in the First Class car. We... I got up, went in there to see what was going on, if I could help.'

'How did you get from your carriage into the First Class car?'

'I tried the connecting door first, but it was locked, so we stepped from our car onto the platform, and then into First Class.'

'The connecting door was locked, you say?'

'Yes.'

Roland licked the tip of his pencil and wrote this into the file.

'And what did you find there?'

'A middle-aged man, short, plump, in formal evening dress – old-fashioned, long coat, that sort of thing – and a young woman, seated, head averted so that she wouldn't see, her hands to her face, sobbing. And the dead man, sitting at the very front of the car.'

'You could see at a glance that he was dead?'

'No, but the situation... it was like some morbid tableau. It seemed immediately obvious.'

'And the other man, where was he, what was he doing?'

'He stood at the front, gazing down on the dead man. He seemed transfixed, as though he couldn't take his eyes off him, and helpless, clearly helpless, utterly deflated... the pose of a man who feels that he must act but doesn't know what to do. I've seen it before at the hospital, when an inexperienced surgeon is faced with some emergency beyond his capability. All it needs is for his senior to step forward and say, "Like this", so I said, "I'm a doctor, let me..." and he snapped out of it and stepped aside to allow me to see.'

'The other couple, were they in the carriage yet?'

167

He thought for a moment or two. 'No, they came after I'd confirmed that the man was dead.'

'How did you do that?'

'Carotid pulse,' his hand moved to his neck in involuntary demonstration, 'pupillary reflex... that face...'

'You've not seen the like before?'

'Oh yes, but only in men brought in with facial burns and head injuries from the front, you know.'

My stomach turned and I'm sure Roland's did the same, both of us having loved ones in immediate danger of such a fate. Roland showed no emotion.

'Then the other couple entered? Where had they come from?'

'I caught a glimpse of someone passing the window, moving along the platform from the front of the train, I saw a face – pale, startled, I thought, looking in, and then they came in. "What's the matter?" the woman said, "can we help?" She went to where Thérèse was trying to comfort the distressed young lady, and the man came to the front with us, to see if there was anything to be done.'

'Did he say anything?'

'No, nothing. He just stood there a moment, taking it in, and then he crouched down, looked up into the dead man's face, looked at both of us, shook his head.'

'And then?'

'The guard came, then the police. We all got off to preserve the scene, is that what you say? I daresay we were all relieved to get out of that atmosphere – it was quite choking.'

'It's exactly what we say, doctor. Thank you very much – you've been a great help.'

'Have I?' The doctor frowned, deep lines for one so young: 'Really?' He looked suddenly weary, infinitely weary.

'Really. The world might be about to change overnight, God help us, but one man's death still matters, and we'll all go on doing our work, eh? Get yourself back to the hospital or, better still, back to that girl of yours. And look after each other.'

After Dr Caron had limped away, Roland gently closed the file and looked up at me, perched on the windowsill with a view of the river and the left bank beyond.

'It's as I thought,' he said. 'We've got this whole thing wrong.'

37

Roland picked up the telephone: 'Clément! Once you've finished scratching your backside, get Nevin to start up the Peugeot, and you wait for us in the Traction Avant in the yard. We're off to the Marais.'

He turned to me, ignoring my openly quizzical expression.

'Who were those two uniforms who were first on the scene?'

'Peres and Picard, you mean?'

'Those are the fellows. See if you can get them over here, pronto.'

From beneath his desk he produced an ox-leather bag.

'Take this to the car with you, would you?'

For its size the bag was surprisingly light. I stood there for a moment, havering, longing to ask what he had meant when he said we had the whole thing wrong.

'Move it, Jojo, and... take your sidearm.'

The two 'woodentops', as Clément derisively called them, rode in the Peugeot with Nevin, while the commissaire and I sat behind Clément in the Traction Avant, leading the way. As we approached Place Saint-Paul, Roland ordered a right turn and within seconds the majestic hood of the Citroën was nosing its way into Rue François Miron, opposite Hôtel de Bergerac.

'Wait here,' Roland demanded as the Peugeot drew up behind us. 'Come on, Jojo.'

Clément watched us as we crossed the road, a sour expression on his face.

'Where are we going, boss?'

'A quick word with Monsieur de Nouaille's little friend.'

'Mademoiselle.. Reski? Won't she be at work?'

'The ministries are all shut. Official Paris has packed and run for it, remember? My daughter went to take her driving test yesterday – no examiners left in the city. The girl will be at home.'

Hôtel de Bergerac reminded me of an aristo gone to seed. Above the once magnificent portal there was a small stone balcony from which the patron of the grand house must once have received his earth-bound petitioners, and rust could not altogether efface the elegance of the scrollwork on the first floor window boxes. Some optimist within had even placed pots of trailing greenery and scarlet geraniums in one of them. This palace was now home to sixty or more families, most of them Jewish, among whom were the Reskis.

In the still magnificent vestibule, which gave onto a weed-infested courtyard, we were met by a slatternly concierge who directed us up the grand staircase to the first floor before returning to her kitchen table, where she was administering the last rites to a bowl of foul-smelling stew in the company of a wizened little chap in a sooty vest, who somehow managed to consume his unappetizing meal with the stub of a cigarette jutting at all times from the corner of his mouth.

The first floor corridor was dark, damp and disconcertingly crunchy underfoot. The smell of stale cooking – not unlike the meal of the concierge and her husband, but with an additional note of gefilte fish – hung in the air and, from somewhere in the depths of this Hadean passage, there was the endless hacking of some poor soul's merciless cough. At the expense of several matches from my fast-depleting supply, we eventually found a door bearing the legend Moishe Reski, Tailleur. Roland knocked.

The Pletzl, or 'Little Place' in Yiddish – an area comprising a few streets around Place Saint-Paul – was

171

in those days a teeming, clamorous centre of industry, but of industry contained within the walls of innumerable family homes. A cramped apartment might host not only the intricate tides of a family's journey through time, but also a manufactory of leather goods or caps, of sweetmeats or ladies' underwear; or the humming, snipping workshop of a tailor.

But not in this case, or no longer. Bolts of cloth were stacked out of the way in a corner, a sewing machine stood idle against a wall, out of the light, and no tape measure hung around the neck of the little man who answered the door to us. Louise Reski peered at us over his head. She had been crying.

Moishe Reski bowed us into the little apartment, for all the world as though he was showing us into some grand establishment on Place Vendôme. As we shook hands he apologised for the absence of his wife, who was presumably scouring the streets for something to cook for dinner or, if she had found an open shop, queueing.

Roland introduced me as 'Inspector Saint-Simon' but the little tailor regarded me with gentle reproof.

'Simon? You're Dr Simon's son aren't you, Monsieur? Such a wonderful gentleman he was, and a scholar too; such a loss. I made all of his suits, right here.'

He made a neat, measured gesture which enlarged that small space to encompass a home, a craftsman's atelier, a shop.

'No more,' he said with a despairing shake of the head, 'there's little call for a bespoke tailor in wartime... not for this one at any rate.'

Looking beyond him to the window I saw the vibrant window box that I had spotted from the street, and felt a strange warm swell of gratitude for this ordinary, anonymous family's homage to life.

'I'll remember you when I need a new suit,' I said, and he beamed in delight, showing teeth notched from a lifetime of pin-holding – the tailor's third hand.

'Monsieur Reski,' said Roland, 'we need a few words with your daughter – to clarify a couple of things, if that's all right?'

'Of course, of course, can I get you anything? Coffee?' He looked around doubtfully, apparently unsure of possessing the means to fulfil his offer of hospitality, and nodded gratefully when Roland politely declined.

'My poor daughter,' he said, reaching out as though to draw her to him.

She took an evasive pace backwards and sat heavily on a small sofa neatly upholstered in navy worsted.

'She has been having such bad dreams, poor girl, crying out at night.'

Mademoiselle Reski pouted in annoyance, shooting her father a look fit to drop him on the spot.

'I didn't see anything. I didn't look after... Why don't you ask Jules... Monsieur de Nouailles, he'd know much better.'

Roland nodded sympathetically.

'Only, we can't locate the gentleman, you see.'

'You're telling me!' She seemed close to tears, and her father alighted softly next to her and began to stroke her hand.

'Well, I expect you know that the government and senior officials have left Paris for an undisclosed location. I doubt he had any choice.'

'I know nothing, he's told me nothing, just gone.'

'I'm sorry,' said Roland, taking one of the chairs at the little dining table and signalling that I, too, should sit. 'Mademoiselle, have you ever heard of the Chevaliers de la France Catholique?'

'No, who are they? Should I have heard of them?'

'I don't think so, necessarily. But Monsieur de Nouailles never mentioned the name, or CFC, CDFC or anything like it?'

'No.' She was positive.

Roland leaned forward and spoke softly: 'Mademoiselle, I am sorry to have to remind you of Monday night...'

She shook her head as though to say, I knew you were here to do this, to carry me back into that nightmare,

'... but, thinking back, were there any signs that M. de Nouailles recognised the victim?'

'How could anyone recognise... that?'

So she had seen. She shivered and passed a hand across her eyes as though seeking to wipe away the memory. Roland extended his hand to her, and she allowed her hand to fall into his. He squeezed it tenderly, like a bear trying not to endanger a precious piece of porcelain.

'Nevertheless?'

'No, there was nothing, I'm sure of it.'

'What about the other men there – the doctor, the Jewish gentleman, the conductor even?'

'No, I'd swear he knew none of them. There was no sign that any of them recognised any of the others – all complete strangers.'

'Ah well,' Roland said as we descended the stairs, 'it seems Monsieur de Nouailles numbered among the respectable, outward faces of the Chevaliers, the useful idiots. If he didn't know the count's top bully boy when he saw him, he's no part of the inner core. Unless,' he paused to consider, 'unless, that is, he's a much better actor than I take him for.'

'Or perhaps he just didn't recognise him – come on, you saw that face.'

'Hmm,' was all he said.

38

We set off in slow procession, directed by Roland towards what I had always regarded as the beating heart of the Pletzl, past the synagogue on rue Pavée, whose threshold I had never crossed, and left into rue des Rosiers. Outside the synagogue only a small group of black-clad men stood in sombre conversation but rue des Rosiers, alone in Paris, retained all its down-at-heel vivacity.

While much of the city had put up the shutters and fled, the Jews of the Pletzl, having no relatives in the countryside, no tradition of holidays by the sea, little sense that they would be welcome elsewhere, had nowhere to go, so they stayed and they carried on.

Despite the morning's filthy drizzle, street-sellers had set out their wares – a tired assortment of carpenters' tools, some outmoded frocks on a rail, a crate of candles, a ripped screen painted with oriental-looking scenes, a pair of brass taps – between the windows of established concerns which were themselves mostly open as usual.

At number 15, Nahoum Goldenberg's restaurant, where my father had liked to go to eat fried fish and play chess, still advertised the dish of the day in the window. At Szlama Goldsztein's épicerie, number 26, a young man in the white coat of a grocer stood at the open door, alternately shaking his head and shrugging as he explained some regrettable fact to a clutch of women on the pavement. And at 36, the boulangerie-patisserie

Moncarz, other women still queued patiently for whatever remained of the day's bread and pastries.

Near the junction with Rue des Écouffes, the same mad young Hassidim paced the same small rectangle of street in which he was always to be found. As ever, he was talking ecstatically to himself or his God, occasionally halting in his tracks and cocking an ear to listen, causing startled pedestrians to skip aside to avert a collision.

All seemed the same as ever, except for the palpable tension, the arid silence where conversation would normally flow, and the drawn, haunted faces.

As we approached the junction with rue des Hospitalières St-Gervais, Roland told Clément to stop. A florist's van, able to pass our funereal procession at last, rattled past over the cobbles and turned into rue Vieille du Temple.

I thought I knew where we were headed now but I couldn't understand why. Roland and I got out of the car and he leaned in to speak quietly to Clément, who nodded his understanding. Then he went to the Peugeot and, with the same discretion, issued orders to Nevin and the two uniformed officers, who tumbled out of the car and walked slowly past me, shouldering their carbines, old Peres tugging gently at the sleeve of his young comrade to maintain the appropriate pace. I watched as they rounded the corner in the eternal plodding manner of policemen on patrol. Nevin drove after them and, as he passed, I could see the flush of excitement on his youthful face.

'Right,' said Roland as he rejoined me, 'you and I are going in.'

'Where?' I asked, though I thought I knew. I noted that he was bringing his old leather bag along and wondered what on earth it could contain.

I was perplexed. 'Surely you can't think the Lederers...'

'You saw her there in Rospeau's café,' he said, though I hadn't known that he had also noticed her. 'What could have taken her over there, to that exact café, except the purchase of black-market diamonds from Rospeau? Portable property, remember? And he was expecting her, wasn't he? She had no trouble getting past my old team-mate on the door, did she? So where did she suddenly come into money? A couple who'd been living in that hovel in the zone, eh?'

He was right. Something had been niggling away at me since I saw her there, and this was it.

Then I understood.

'You mean...'

I thought for a long moment, my incredulity blown apart by the incontrovertible fact. They had had nothing.

'You mean someone paid them to kill Thomas Fabricant?'

I was thinking quickly now, the inevitable truth flooding through the door that he had flung open before me.

'The family of Thomas's girl... they'd tracked Thomas to Paris, then they found a man down on his luck – a fellow Czech Jew – perhaps they even knew where to find him... a big man, a strong man, a man desperate enough to do anything to haul himself and his wife out of the midden, yes... I see it now.'

Roland glanced at me, one bushy eyebrow raised and a faint smile on his lips.

'So they paid cash,' I continued, 'but at least part of it only when the deed was done, and the cash had to be converted into, as you say, "portable property." That's it.'

'So why didn't he go to complete the deal with Rospeau? Why risk his wife getting robbed on the way home? You saw how nervous possession of the money and the diamonds made young Lévy, right?'

I was still pondering this when we turned the corner and there was Clément, sitting in the Traction Avant, puffing away on his pipe and pretending to consult a road atlas. We went on to stand for a few moments on the corner with rue des Francs Bourgeois. Peres and Picard were enacting a meticulous little drama of inspecting the Peugeot, which was parked across the road from the restaurant. Of Nevin there was no sign.

'We've been idiots from the start of this,' Roland said suddenly. 'This was never about politics or war or gangland crime. This was always about love. I should have seen that before now.'

He set off at a brisk clip across the road with me at his heels, and shouldered his way through the open door of Rozenstroikh's restaurant.

In the Pletzl, cafés and restaurants had long been the social clubs and labour exchanges for particular trades. You arrived as a stranger to the city and someone would soon tell you to seek the advice of Wolf Speiser at his bookshop in rue des Rosiers. We had passed it on our way, and I had been saddened to observe the decay into which it had fallen, for Wolf was old now and ailing.

If you happened to be a tailor or a furrier or a cap-maker; or a silver or goldsmith for that matter, Wolf Speiser would recommend that you visit Rozenstroikh's, and there, over a bowl of cabbage borscht, you might meet a man who knew a man who had heard of a vacancy suitable for you.

In common with most Jews in the city, I had not yet committed fully to the truth that this was a world that was about to end.

The afternoon being well advanced, only a few old men lingered over weak beer and coffee in the restaurant, a group of four playing a roisterous round of pinochle and a more contemplative pair by the window at the backgammon board. These undemanding and unprofitable few requiring little attention, a solitary waiter in a long white apron and yarmulke presided. He lowered his eyes as we approached him, while the card-players, eyes bright and inquisitive above full white beards, grew quiet as they followed our progress. It was clear that everyone knew exactly what we were. Only the clatter of the dice disturbed the sudden silence.

Roland spoke quietly to the waiter, who was himself an elderly man with a lemony pallor, sad brown eyes, and chasmic lines framing his downturned mouth and creasing his forehead, as though he had already seen all the suffering there ever was to be in this world. He spoke little French so Roland summoned me forward to speak to him in Yiddish.

'Upstairs,' he said in answer to my question, 'they're upstairs resting before the evening service – second floor, end of the landing.'

Nevin popped his head round the courtyard door as we entered the stairwell.

'Ready, boss,' he said, tapping the butt of the pistol in his waistband.

He still had the look of a kid whose birthday has come unexpectedly early, simultaneously excited and jittery. The image of the aspen leaves shivering and dancing in the breeze came suddenly to mind.

Roland and I began to climb the stairs.

Roland put down his bag and knocked on the door as lightly as the old man downstairs might, apologetic about disturbing them during their break. I drew my automatic and stood back, levelling it at the middle of the door.

The door opened a crack and Roland was through it, his bulk and speed overwhelming whoever was behind the door and sending them crashing to the floor.

'Police judiciaire,' I yelled and stepped into the room.

Bare boards and peeling wallpaper with the fading memory of a floral pattern; a wooden chair piled with clothing beside a metal-framed single bed and, in the bed, Madame Lederer, one slim bare leg exposed by the turning aside of the sheet.

She clutched the sheet around her to cover her nakedness and her mouth was opened in a soundless scream. Her unscarfed neck bore livid witness to a recent attempt at strangulation, the bruises left by two large, strong hands closing around her throat. I kept her covered with the Star Ruby held in both hands, arms extended.

'Stay there,' I commanded, quite unnecessarily since she seemed paralysed by terror.

On the floor, Roland had Lederer face down and was applying the handcuffs. A twenty centimetre chef's knife glinted at the foot of the wall beneath the window, where the force of Roland's charge had propelled it. Satisfied, Roland lumbered to his feet, dragging the other upright in front of him.

Lederer wore only a pair of briefs and his nose was never going to recover its noble profile after its recent encounter with door or floor but, even with his arms manacled behind him, he appeared defiant and capable – tall, lean and muscular, his dark eyes on the move, weighing the situation for opportunity.

Then his gaze settled on me, on the pistol I pointed at his woman, and his handsome features twisted in sudden fury. He strained to lunge at me but Roland held him without apparent effort and spoke in a calm and soothing voice.

'We've been looking everywhere for you, Tomáš, not that we knew it, but we got there in the end and it's all over now.'

180

Tomáš? I felt momentarily unbalanced, as though the solid floor beneath my feet had become suddenly unmoored and set adrift. Tomáš? If this was Tomáš Weil then who had been murdered on a Line One train on Monday evening?

Then I saw it.

Roland led his captive to the door and reached into the bag on the floor outside.

'This is yours, I believe.'

He placed the brown fedora on the other's head. It was a perfect fit.

39

'Congratulations,' I said to Roland as we resumed our habitual positions in his office, 'but when did you know? How?'

'I won't have congratulations in a capital case,' he rebuked me, his large face solemn, 'not when two young people face the guillotine because of me.'

'No, not because of you. Because they conspired to murder an inconvenient husband. When did you know?'

He shook his head slowly. 'Seeing her in Rospeau's café, knowing she could be there for one purpose only... And yet the Lederers had no money, nothing, it made no sense.

'It was then that I thought back to the question of identification. We had a faceless man with no ID on him and I thought, how did we identify him?

'Answer, we established his identity ourselves, through a smart bit of police work. We found the ticket on him and assumed the killer had overlooked it – such a little thing, and people don't imagine they're traceable. Then we found the woman who'd sold him the tickets and, through what we learned from her, we found someone who had a full name and address for him, and the rest followed.

'If we'd found an ID card on him we might have considered the possibility that it was a fake, a plant, but no, we went and established his identity for ourselves like good detectives are supposed to, so we were totally committed to it.

'He's a clever fellow, Monsieur Weil, and he knows how the minds of investigators work, so he threw us this one little clue, just tempting enough that we were bound to swallow it – and congratulate our stupid selves for snapping it up.

'So, after we'd re-interviewed the first people on the scene, taking us back, if you like, to that night in the Métro car, I thought, what if we're wrong? If it wasn't Thomas Fabricant – Tomáš Weil – then who is it? And what do the Lederers, who've mysteriously come into money, have to do with it? And if they did have any involvement, why would they reboard the First Class carriage when the body's discovered? They could easily just walk on and out of the station, and we'd never have found them. We heard it from Dr Caron – Lederer crouched to look up into that destroyed face, why?'

'Because he needed to be sure that the acid had done its work,' I said in a rush of enthusiasm for his theory. 'He had to know that the face was unidentifiable. Another thing – what is it Prof de Chevigny likes to say? "Every contact leaves a trace." They made sure they were seen in the carriage after the discovery of the body to account for any evidence of their presence before the killing.'

'Exactly. And then there was the question of why Lederer sent his woman to buy the diamonds. Such a risky errand. Rospeau might just take their money, or she might be followed and robbed on the way home. It only made sense if he couldn't go. Because Rospeau knew him, and not as Alfred Lederer.

'You came up with an explanation for their involvement, Jojo, and it wasn't a bad effort, but no. There could only be one answer.

'I suddenly remembered the fellow's hat being too small for him, something I'd written off as another sign of his poverty, but then I got it. The hat was too small because it wasn't his, the man beneath the hat wasn't Alfred Lederer. The hats had been swapped. The men had been swapped.

183

'And it was all about the woman after all, Madame Lederer was Tomáš's girl from back home. He must have found her there in the zone while he was doing his penance – fate, eh? – and everything followed from that.

'We heard a few things about her husband – a violent, controlling, drunken parasite. He'd never let her go, he'd kill her first. Maybe he had a go – you saw the marks of strangulation on her neck – so if Tomáš wanted his girl and she wanted him, there was only one way. And if Tomáš was to have his woman – his Jewish woman – he had to go all in; take a bit of money but leave everything else behind, disappear. Better, cease to exist so that no one would be looking for him.'

'And who's more invisible in Paris these days than a pair of poor refugees, another couple of Jews fled from faraway to the Pletzl?' I said, thrilled by his reasoning.

From the window I could see the residual trickle of weary refugees trudging across Pont Saint-Michel, insensible to the resumption of the oily drizzle.

Nevin entered. I had been so absorbed in the rapid re-evaluation of all that I'd heard and seen in the course of the investigation that I had been deaf to his knock.

'The male suspect says he wants to talk to you, boss,' said Nevin.

'Ha! He's learned French now, has he?' said Roland, flapping a hand to indicate that Nevin should bring Weil to him.

'Wait a minute!' I said, suddenly recognising an anomaly. 'Who on earth was having us watched?'

'Good question.' He smiled, 'But if you're worried about the girl – what's her name... Mademoiselle Mulot – don't be, I've had her moved. She's back at your place, by the way.'

'What?'

'Your young lady said it would be fine. The watchers seem to have been called off and, if anyone is still looking for her, it's the last place they'll think of.'

The door opened and Tomáš Weil, Thomas Fabricant, the man who had posed as Alfred Lederer in his shabby suit and undersized Homburg, stood there in manacles. But this was no cowed refugee. This man was unmistakably a warrior.

40

'I'll tell you everything,' he said, 'just let Myriam go – she did nothing.'

He appeared perfectly at ease, sitting forward on the plywood chair reserved for suspects and witnesses, his manacled hands folded on the desk in front of him. I pulled up a chair and sat at the end of the desk, ready to transcribe his confession.

'The juge d'instruction will decide about that but I can make recommendations,' Roland replied, leaning forward with his great hands folded on the blotter, mirroring the man he was to question. 'Let's hear what you've got to say. We assume that Madame Lederer is the girl you'd loved back at home – only her family didn't approve and chased you off. That right?'

'So you know about that – yes, that's broadly right.'

Momentarily his face had the look of one who is forced to swallow bitter medicine. Shame? Guilt? Humiliation? All three perhaps.

'Later, I heard about her being married off to Lederer – he's the son of a rival of her father's, so it was like one of those old dynastic marriages, you know, peace bought on the body of your daughter. They really were a bunch of bastards...

'Anyway, when the Germans came in '38 – Teplice-Šanov, where our families lived, was in the part of Bohemia where most people speak German – Myriam knew there was no future for her there, so she persuaded Lederer that they must leave. He was still besotted with her then and imagined that if he went along with it he could yet win her round, I suppose, so they got a train to Dresden and then to Budapest. That was no good so they came to Paris, where things weren't much better.

'I think he'd got the message by then – she was never going to love him, not even respect him – and his drinking worsened. Myriam would go out every day and find whatever work she could – cleaning, cooking, waitressing – and he'd just lie in that filthy hut and drink.'

'Yes, in the zone near Porte de Vincennes. That's where you found her again, wasn't it?'

Weil's hands opened on the desk, fingers splayed like a card player folding.

'You already know it all.'

'Not all, carry on.'

'I spotted her there about three months ago. She looked so miserable, she'd lost weight, aged. It was... unbearable. But I couldn't show myself and heap my misery onto her. She had to come to me... she had to want to come with me.'

'You still loved her.'

'Love her. That has no end.'

Tears had formed in his eyes. He brought his manacled hands up to wipe them away and took a few seconds to compose himself.

'An old woman, the widow of a furrier, whose house Myriam cleaned every week told her about jobs going in Rozenstroikh's, so she went over there and convinced them to take her and her husband as a pair and let them a room into the bargain – that's how she is – and she even persuaded him that it would be a new start for them. They were to move in the next Monday and start work on the Tuesday.'

'I see,' Roland sat back, tapping his teeth with a pencil, a habit of his that was beginning to irritate me. 'Which of you came up with the idea of killing him en route, so that you could turn up at the restaurant as her husband?'

Weil's hands clenched tightly on the desk.

187

'I did that, alone. She knew nothing about that.'

'Really?' Roland's eyes were fixed on the unimpeachable blotter, as though seeking an undiscovered stain. 'What about the suit? What about the First Class tickets that you bought? How did Monsieur Lederer come by those?'

We had evidently arrived at the point that Weil had been dreading. Sweat broke on his forehead and trickled down onto his crushed nose.

'Look, Myriam came to me, she said they'd got these jobs but he had nothing respectable to wear. That's when the idea came to me, so clearly it was luminous. I gave her one of my old suits, told her to say it was from the old woman she worked for – one of her late husband's.'

'Lederer was a big man but, even so, I reckon your suit would come up a bit too big for him...'

'I got a tailor I know to alter it – a favour – to something more like his size, said it was for a friend.'

Roland sat in silence for a while, frowning, pursing his lips, and shaking that great head.

'And I bought them the tickets, yes, First Class because there was every chance that car would be empty right up to Hôtel de Ville or beyond. If it could be done on the train, I planned to get her off and onto a different car at Gare de Lyon, and then off at Saint-Paul leaving the body to travel on and away from us.'

'Where did you get on?'

'Nation.'

'And by Gare de Lyon you'd killed your lady's husband, won her round to your plan, poured acid over the victim's face, swapped hats with him and got her composed enough to get off the train with you, and back on again a couple of cars away?'

188

'Well, the crowds at Gare de Lyon were a problem, but they did provide cover. No one was going to notice any individual or couple in that press...'

'All that in, what, three or four minutes?'

'I'm trained, a professional...'

'Yes, we heard about that.'

'That too?'

I looked up and claimed his gaze. 'You'd be surprised how much we know.'

He nodded and moistened his lips.

Roland resumed, 'Talk us through the killing itself.'

'I got on at Nation, saw that they were in the front seats – good – and he was dozing – even better – probably drunk. I stepped up behind him, stuck him with the ice pick, gathered up Myriam, hushed her, told her not to look, poured the acid over his face, left the icepick and bottle, that was it. Thirty seconds.'

'You've used this ice pick method before?'

'Oh yes – special duties, you understand, in the Legion. The weapon is easily acquired and simple to explain away, death is instant and leaves no obvious wound and little blood, and the victim looks like a man who's dozed off – gives you time to get away.'

Roland nodded understandingly and then leaned forward abruptly, so that their heads came close to a collision. Weil flinched involuntarily.

'What would you have done if anyone else had been in the First Class car?'

'I'd have trailed Myriam and her "husband" into the Pletzl – I'm trained and well-practised, remember? – and I'd have found an opportunity somewhere in those narrow streets and alleys.'

Roland sighed, sat back in his chair and tucked that damned pencil behind his ear, all with the air of one entirely satisfied.

'Thank you, M. Weil. We'll have your statement typed, ready for signing.'

He signalled that Weil should stand and I opened the door to admit Nevin, his escort.

As Nevin was about to close the door behind them, Roland sniffed loudly and said in a casual, gentle tone, 'Monsieur, why do you suppose Madame Lederer had led her drunken husband all the way to the front seats? Surely it would have been easier to settle him near the entrance?'

41

Myriam Lederer sat on the chair recently vacated by her lover, hands folded calmly in her lap as though she faced nothing more taxing than a round of belote. I watched her from my perch on the windowsill, notebook in hand. She was a beauty, all right – courageous too – and it was easy to see how any man might fall for her.

Unconfined, her black hair flowed to below the shoulders and framed a pale, oval face enhanced, if anything by the absence of make-up. Dark half-moons beneath her eyes spoke of the strain she had been under, and the bruises on her neck of the tyranny she had endured.

To love her, yes; to want her, definitely, but to kill and perhaps to die for that love? I couldn't dismiss the idea unreservedly, though I do not consider myself a romantic, still less a sentimentalist.

Roland sat forward, elbows on the desk and bucket hands folded beneath his chin as he regarded her, tenderness in his eyes. When he spoke to her his voice was soft, slow and undemanding, like a dairyman addressing his favourite cow. He knew that she had suffered greatly, he said, and thought it likely that she was, in part, relieved that it was all over. He wondered if she would like to tell him all about it.

She turned her head and looked at me, a faint faraway smile on her lips but not in her eyes, which seemed to see through and beyond me to some other reality, like the eyes of a sleepwalker. Finally, she turned back to Roland.

'What did he tell you? What did Tomàš say?' Her voice seemed to come to us from a great distance, as though she already spoke from the underworld.

To my great surprise, Roland answered frankly, offering her a way out.

'Monsieur Weil took full and sole responsibility for the death of your husband, Madame. He insists that you played no part in the murder of Monsieur Lederer.'

A sigh escaped her: 'I knew he would lie.'

She met Roland's silent and sorrowful gaze.

'It is untrue. When a miracle happened, when Tomàš and I found each other among a continent full of people on the move, I knew that I could not bear to be apart from him ever again. And I knew that Alfred would never let me go – he would kill me first.'

A hand went to her neck, where the bruises were still livid.

'So I said to Tomàš that our only recourse was to kill him.'

'Could you not have simply run away together, madame?'

She appeared suddenly stunned, as if the idea had never occurred to her. After a while she gathered herself sufficiently to reply.

'I need to be Tomàš's wife. I couldn't be his wife as long as Alfred lived.'

'Did Monsieur Lederer know that you had found Tomàš, or that he had found you?'

'He suspected that something had happened, but he was always suspecting that.'

Absently, she rubbed the bruises again.

'I had been looking for work with accommodation, so that we could, at least, escape that place where my husband's despair and rage grew day by day, and then I heard about Rozenstroikh's and went to see the owner. My husband even thought I must have been with a lover that afternoon, but I showed him a letter from the owner, offering him work as a kitchen porter, me as a waitress, and a room of our own, and eventually he believed me.'

Her French was slow, methodical and correct, like that of a diligent schoolgirl.

'And then... and then I went to see the doctor to get some cream of arnica for the bruises, and there − I couldn't believe it − sitting in Dr Descoups' seat... there was Tomàš.'

Her eyes closed as she relived the scene.

'It was like a dream... it was a miracle,' she breathed.

So they constructed their plan, using the materials and circumstances to hand: Tomàš Weil's best suit − not at all some old cast-off − to dress the would-be kitchen porter, and the offer of a job with accommodation.

Alfred Lederer would leave the zone with his wife one evening and would arrive at Rozenstroikh's restaurant in a new, much improved package, albeit in a shabbier suit, while a sadly degraded Tomàš Weil, aka Thomas Fabricant, would continue his last, solitary journey in First Class, it was to be hoped to the end of the line.

'How did you persuade your husband to travel in First Class?' I asked.

'He took no persuading at all. He took it as his right. He wouldn't think to question such a thing. Besides, he was half drunk − I made sure of that.'

'Tomàš gave you the tickets?'

She nodded.

'And I led my husband to the station and onto the First Class carriage. I took him to the front seats because that is what we had agreed I should do. That way, when Tomáš boarded the train, he would be behind Alfred.'

'That's not what he said,' Roland offered.

'I am sure it is not − because he wants to take it all on himself and save me. But I do not want to be saved if he is to suffer death. We planned it together and did it together – I took my "husband" by the hand and led him to his death, and I regret nothing. I will not consent to live without the man I love any longer.'

Her dark-eyed gaze did not shift from Roland's. His eyes dropped but hers held fast.

'I'm sorry, madame—'

'I'm sure it won't come to that,' I interrupted, unable to restrain myself.

Roland's eyebrows rose almost imperceptibly but I continued.

'Your husband's violent behaviour—'

The door swung open and I gaped up at the intruders. Commissaire Xavier Six materialised in the room, a grinning Gaspard Raban in his wake and, behind him, an apologetic Nevin, positively wringing his hands in contrition. The woman, unflinching, continued to stare at Roland.

'A word, if I may, Commissaire Roland,' said Six, removing an imaginary fleck from the front of his suit jacket.

'So that's it,' said Roland, nodding as though to remind himself that he had always known.

42

'I thought you said you were leaving Paris last night, Xavier,' said Roland.

We were ranged around his office, freshly brewed coffee too hot to drink yet on the desk, three of us smoking – in Six's case a noxious little Dannemann cigar – and Roland lounging in his big old chair, relieved to have removed the chafing celluloid collar from his shirt, and looking like a farm hand home from Sunday mass. Our prisoners waited in their separate cells to learn their fate.

'Yes, well, Monsieur Langeron did suggest that all intelligence officers should remove themselves from Paris and I would have, but...'

'You had something on, an operation,' suggested Roland.

'You understand my dilemma perfectly.'

'You had agents in the field and you couldn't leave until you knew the outcome.'

Six nodded fervently. 'Exactly so.'

'And that would be us. My team, your unwitting assets.'

I had to grip the windowsill to prevent myself from falling from the open window. Six, upright in one of the plywood chairs reserved for suspects, maintained an affable silence, puffing away on that damned cigarillo.

'We were the operation and its goal was to find your runaway agent. That's why you were on surveillance in Rue Mesnil, wasn't it – Tomáš, Thomas, Tom Pouce, call him what you will, hadn't shown for a rendezvous or something; I don't know, maybe he'd run off with the Bureau's party fund, but he was missing and you were worried he'd been blown.'

'It was a concern, yes. The people he had been involved with on our behalf...'

'The Comte de l'Île and his Chevaliers de la France Catholique?'

A moue of distaste appeared fleetingly on Six's face.

'Indeed. Contrary to any impression I may have given during our encounter in Rue Mesnil, they represented a grave and novel threat to the security of the Republic, of the nation itself. They were certainly in treasonous communication with the enemy, and they had no qualms about murdering their enemies or anyone suspected of disloyalty to their so-called cause. In fact,' he added, paying close attention to the glowing tip of his cigar, 'Tomàš was the count's favourite assassin. He made three individuals disappear completely – safely into our protective custody, you understand – and killed two "traitors" to the Chevaliers, senior chaps, vital cogs in their machine. Pity, really.

'So, yes, when he failed to show up we feared the worst, but when you showed us your scene of crime snaps,' he looked at Raban, who ran his hand through his mop of mousey hair and smiled broadly at me, 'we saw immediately that it wasn't him – your man had a small area of baldness on the crown, our man had a full head of hair – so we knew he wasn't dead but running. We needed to bring him in, but no longer had the manpower to do it. Who better to find him than Paris's finest detective? That's what the papers call you, is it not?'

'And now we have him – bang to rights on a murder charge.'

Roland removed the pencil from behind his ear and, instead of drumming and tapping with it, began to chew on its end – which was a welcome innovation.

'Oh, I don't think we have to proceed with that, do we? I have an aeroplane waiting to take him away to

196

England with us. Weigh his crime in the balance against the service he can do France in the future – a man like him is worth more than his weight in gold in wartime.'

'After all, what's one dead Jew more or less...?' Raban interjected.

My stomach lurched but I hesitated, thinking it a clumsy piece of sarcasm, an old vice of Raban's, but Roland was on his feet and reaching for him with his left hand while a piledriver of a fist formed in the other. Raban tried to back away, hands raised in apology and face drained of all colour. His chair toppled backwards and he ended in a tangle on the floor, banging his head on the bookcase in the process.

'We'll have none of that, Gaspard,' said Six, calmly lighting another cigarillo, his quick eyes on me, his head inclining to show regret.

'I think he was being sarcastic, boss,' I said to calm my commissaire.

'Don't be,' Roland eyed Raban with distaste, the heat still high on his cheeks.

'Look,' said Six, unfolding his legs and fastidiously flicking ash into the ashtray on the desk. 'You're worrying about the investigating magistrate...'

'Leclerc,' Roland grunted.

Another moue of distaste.

'Well, it would be, wouldn't it? Tell him the perpetrator took his own life – it has the virtue of a certain poetic truth, after all. Who's to know? Thomas Fabricant is dead – that's an established fact with all who need to know – and Alfred Lederer? Who in France even knew of the man's existence?'

'I'm a prose man, myself, and I like my facts to be verifiably true. And I know of Monsieur Lederer's existence... and the manner of his death.'

Roland stared into the imperturbable features of his fellow commissaire, and I could see the emotion rising in him, anger in the set of that jaw, the lowering eyebrows.

'Did you know that your agent was seeing a psychiatrist?' he asked, forcibly calming his voice.

Six waved this away, wafting a ring of pungent smoke in my direction and away through the window.

'Not a problem – I knew that Fabricant would never disclose any operational information. Besides, Lefèvre was security-cleared, and if it helped Thomas to remain operationally effective...'

Roland shifted forward in his seat. I hoped I wouldn't have to attempt to restrain him because I knew I would fail.

'Well, he stopped going – did you know that?' he said through clenched teeth.

Six considered this intelligence without a muscle in his face moving.

'Did you know that?' Roland repeated, 'You didn't, did you? But you'd taken a man already broken by the crimes – yes, I said crimes – he'd committed for France, and you sent him out to do it all again. What do you think that's done to him, eh? And now you're telling me that you're going to make him carry on doing it? For God's sake, look at yourself, Xavier, will you?'

His anger had blown itself out and he now seemed overcome by a titanic sorrow at the plight of humanity. 'Will you?'

'All right.'

Six conjured a pocket watch from somewhere about his person and shot a glance at its face.

'Time's running on and the electricity is being cut at nightfall, and the Germans will own the city by morning. Those are the material facts as of this moment. In prose. Verifiable.'

He produced a letter from an inner pocket.

'I had hoped to avoid involving his name in this, but you ever were a righteous and stubborn old thing, Arthur, so you'd better read this before the lights go out.'

He held the letter out to Roland, who accepted it reluctantly into his paw. I saw that it was addressed to him, marked 'For Your Eyes Only', and written in a neat, small hand, although a certain frugality in recourse to the blotter suggested some haste. Roland read slowly and deliberately, and then reread. At last he was satisfied.

'Match?' he demanded, and then set light to the page, watching as it was reduced to a fine ash in the ashtray.

'I take it you agree that that outranks and supersedes your commission rogatoire and Citizen Leclerc to boot?'

Roland sighed volcanically. 'You'll have to take his woman because, if I've got him right, he'll go nowhere without her.'

Six considered this carefully, as though he were mapping the precise logistical requirements of his latest illusion.

'So be it. He's worth it,' he said at last.

'Then we're agreed,' Roland sighed in resignation, 'except for one last thing. Who was keeping you informed on every step in this investigation? Clément... Nevin... Jojo here?'

He looked at me with sorrow in his eyes and I felt suddenly sick, unaccountably guilty.

'No, not you.'

I breathed again.

Xavier Six, 'Double X', just shrugged and turned to go. The lights went out as he closed the door gently behind them.

'What was it that young neurologist said?' Roland sighed.

I was momentarily puzzled, but then remembered Dr Caron's parting shot about the frustrating impotence of his profession – all diagnosis and no treatment. 'That's us, all right,' I admitted. 'This time.'

43

The next morning was bright, clear and warm, like a new beginning.

I do not remember what clothes I threw on that morning. I guess I picked up whatever came first to hand – yesterday's shirt, suit and shoes perhaps – only ensuring that my socks, vest and underpants were fresh from the laundry. Certain standards, after all, lie beyond our power to breach them, deriving from the primal dread communicated by the universal mother – that of having her son found dead in the street in unclean underpants.

I left the two women breakfasting on fruit, stale bread and coffee in a sombre semi-silence, catching each other's eye from time to time in sudden, shared apprehension. I had gulped down my own coffee like a mute automaton, neither tasting it nor feeling its heat on my tongue and palate.

I was late.

On my way to 36 I had intended to cross Place de l'Hôtel de Ville but the sudden sight of the swastika standard, flying over the seat of my city's government in the rightful place of the Tricolore stunned me.

According to my father the swastika is a symbol with its origins in deepest antiquity, and it was in ancient times associated with ideas of the oneness of creation, of peace, good fortune and well-being. Now it bore very different connotations. Here, it was a statement that the Germans had wasted no time in asserting their dominance over Paris, and it was altogether too much for me.

It was as though I had stepped unwary into the street and been hit by a truck. I stopped dead, as though winded, and tried to take in the unbelievable scene. A great banner bearing the despicable device hung above the main entrance of the Hôtel de Ville, a blight on that dignified façade, a wen on the face of republican virtue.

A group of armoured vehicles, sombrely painted in camouflage of dark grey and deep brown, had drawn up on the parvis, and around them milled jubilant soldiers in field grey; tall, blonde and ridiculously handsome. A pair of young Parisiennes in summer frocks stood by, open in their admiration and exchanging the odd sly, suggestive remark with the men. I decided to go the other way.

In Place du Châtelet, I paused beside the du Palmier Fountain and lit a cigarette, my first of the day, gazing up with melancholic irony at the gilded figure of Victory, glittering satirically against the clear blue sky. Both of the great theatres were closed, dark and silent; solemn monuments to an age that had suddenly passed, to a city from which light had been banished.

I could hear the continuous rumble and roar of a mechanised army passing through Paris somewhere in the distance, but here the war had been settled. Outside the only open café on the square, figures in field grey – tall, blonde, handsome – lounged at the tables, exhaustion and elation on their faces as they bantered over brandy and beer from the bottle. They insisted on paying, I noticed, but the patron looked as though he did not know what was to be done with their unfamiliar currency.

Loudspeaker vans were touring the streets, ordering the civilian population to remain indoors for forty-eight hours while the German army passed through, but a few intrepid or foolish or compulsively curious souls had ventured out and now stood around, in silent groups or alone, watching the German soldiers with the fearful admiration with which one might regard a pack of wolves, escaped from the menagerie and now conducting itself with surprising decorum in the streets of the city.

A detachment of troops passed in formation, followed by an officer seated in the back of an open-topped car. The car stopped and the officer stood and began to address the little crowd in French. I looked at my watch – 09.20 – and decided to hear what he had to say, so that I might report it to Roland on arrival at 36.

'Your great and proud nation,' he was saying, 'has been very badly governed. It is beyond rational understanding that France declared war on Germany when we sought only the place in world affairs that is rightfully ours. In this, we have only ever wanted the same as your allies, the English. Well, they have betrayed and abandoned you now, and no harm will come to you at our hands – nothing bad will happen to anyone. Once there is peace again between Germany and France, we shall deal with England within a fortnight, you will see.'

He surveyed his audience, nodding, a thin smile on his lips, exuding self-belief. Finally satisfied that he had achieved the effect he desired, he sat down, replaced his braided cap, and gave the order to drive on.

By the time I arrived at 36 – past machine gun posts at every corner of the Préfecture, cafés filled with figures in field grey, others where elderly Parisians stubbornly took their morning coffee and cognac at tables alongside groups of guffawing invaders – my heart was pounding, my palms were sweating, and my brain felt as though it had been scooped out of its case and replaced with cotton wool. Nothing seemed real. The world seemed suddenly separated from me by an unbreakable sheet of glass.

Clément and Nevin were already at their desks in the aquarium. Nevin, usually so industrious, just sat there, head in hands, but Clément looked up as I entered and cocked an eyebrow.

'Christ, Simon, what time do you call this? The boss has been asking for you.'

I looked at my watch – 09.45 – and then saw that Clément was pointing at the big clock on the wall – 10.45. I looked at my watch again, the dreadful feeling of unreality swelling until it seemed that I must be about to go mad. I sat heavily in my chair.

'Don't worry, cock,' Clément's voice came to me from across oceans, 'we're on Berlin time now. Orders.'

I shook my head – this could not be real, this had to be a nightmare from which I would soon awake.

Clément was still talking, shouting now, it seemed to me: 'I hope you've handed in your sidearm.' His crude features wore a smug, triumphant leer.

'What?'

'Your handgun, have you handed it in?'

I felt for it, its reassuring bulk, heavy with responsibility, beneath my left armpit. 'No, why?'

He whistled: 'Fuck me, you're lucky you weren't stopped and searched – they'd have put you up against the nearest wall and shot you. They're all over the place, aren't they? Knowing exactly which buildings they want, every government office, every fucking street corner they want a signpost on. The boss walked in past Rue des Saussaies – says they're already there, turning the place inside-fucking-out looking for files.'

So they were in the Central Bureau of Intelligence's offices. I hoped nothing had been left for them to find.

'Jojo, I need you for a moment.'

Roland filled the doorway. Silently, I got up to follow him.

'Better leave your gun with me,' said Clément. 'I'll call down to the armoury.'

'You all right, kid?' Roland asked solicitously as he led the way to his office. 'Kid'. He'd never called me that before. 'You look like you've seen a ghost.'

'Clément's right, they're everywhere,' I said, 'overnight, just like that. And they're all so bloody tall and blond and handsome...'

'Not all,' he said, opening the door.

44

A short, rotund man in field grey stood as we entered. Mid-forties, I estimated, with a smooth plump face, bakelite-framed spectacles balanced on a nose that resembled a blob of putty, and a rim of reddish hair around a hemisphere of naked crown. I could not make out the meaning of the insignia on his tunic.

'Aha,' he said pleasantly, 'So you must be the famous Inspector Joseph Simon...'

'Saint-Simon,' Roland corrected him.

'Ah yes, my mistake. I have heard a lot about you, Inspector.'

Intelligent, milky blue eyes appraised me from behind thick lenses that so magnified them that I had the sensation of beholding some far greater and mightier creature contained within his insignificant form. He bowed stiffly at the waist and held out a hand for me to shake. I ignored it.

'Already?' I said sardonically.

He let his hand drop but his eyes remained on me, betraying no sign that offence had been taken.

'Hauptmann Walther Jäger of the Feldgendarmerie,' he introduced himself.

So his insignia were those of a military policeman. He didn't look like one.

'Commissaire Roland and I are old colleagues,' he said, causing me to look sharply at Roland in surprise, 'so of course I have heard about his most trusted inspector. May I ask if you speak German, Inspector?'

I almost blurted out, 'Only Yiddish', but managed to stop myself. The sensation of being in the midst of a bad dream remained with me.

'No,' I said, 'I'm sorry.'

'Sorry.' Was politeness to the enemy a betrayal? At that moment I felt it was. Was this seemingly affable man my enemy? He did not immediately feel like one. It was confusing.

'Ah well,' he said, 'In that case, I shall have to continue in my execrable French.' His French was near-perfect, the accent possibly Swiss.

'We worked together in Berlin,' Roland said. 'That case I told you about.'

He hadn't told me about it at the time. He'd returned in an uncharacteristically morose mood and had discussed it with no one except, I imagine, the Chief. The first time I'd heard him say anything about it had been in the last few days.

Jäger sat and signalled that we should do likewise. It was clear who was in control here.

'These are difficult times for you, I can understand that.'

He took a cigarette case from his pocket and offered it around. We both declined. He lit up – an American brand, I thought, from the aroma.

'But this is the awkward situation in which we find ourselves...'

'Awkward situation?' I blurted. 'You've invaded our fucking country!'

Suddenly he did feel like the enemy after all. He only shrugged and knocked a little ash off – carefully, into the ash tray.

'And you declared war on mine. It is what it is, and we must make the best of it and work together. Think of it, the only two great cultures in Europe, Germany and France, in time, united.'

He was nodding and smiling. I was thinking of Russia, Italy, Greece... but I said, 'Only two great cultures? What about the English, for one?'

He laughed and slapped the table: 'The English? The English don't have a culture, they have jokes about bodily functions.'

Roland maintained a ponderous silence, sitting deep in his chair and chewing the end of a pencil.

'Look, I am here to help,' said Jäger. 'To mediate between your department and the new authorities and perhaps,' he looked suddenly eager, 'to do a little real police work.'

'You could start by getting us our arms back,' I said under Roland's slow gaze.

'You have been disarmed? How ridiculous. I didn't know but, now that I do, I shall see that the measure is reversed by tonight. I know that the General has been entirely satisfied with the conduct of the people and police of Paris so far, entirely satisfied. I think you will find that the forty-eight hour curfew will also be rescinded by tonight although, regrettably, there will be a 21.00 curfew thereafter.'

'I see,' said Roland.

After the German had gone, repeating his promise to have our sidearms returned, Roland sighed and closed his eyes for a moment, holding the root of his nose between two thick fingers as though to prevent a sneeze.

'He was a good copper, Walther, and a decent enough bloke compared to some of them, but...' He left it hanging there. 'Take the weekend off, Jojo. You could do with a break. But make sure you incinerate the Fabricant-Weil file before you go.'

'Double-X took it, boss. I thought you knew.'

'For God's sake, take these with you,' he said, reaching into the drawer for the papers he had obtained for me. I took them: my family's new history.

45

I took him at his word and took the weekend off. Ammarah's venues had not yet reopened and Louise Mulot had felt bold enough to return to her little apartment, so we spent a rare weekend together. It was a perfect summer weekend too. At night we defied the stifling heat and made love, and by day we visited our favourite places.

We strolled through the Tuileries gardens, where the cafés were filled with field grey – yes, on that second day of the occupation it was still possible for an atheistic Jew and his mixed-race lover to walk hand in hand in the public parks under the lustily appreciative gaze of German troops – and we basked in the hot sun on the bank of the Seine on the Île de la Cité. We took the Métro to Porte Maillot and lunched on the terrace of a bistro before wandering around in the Bois de Boulogne pretending to get lost, and gradually the feeling of unreality lifted from me.

Paris was occupied but it was still Paris, and I was still in love with the city, and with Ammarah too. I knew that now.

On Monday I returned to 36, determined to carry on as normally as possible – Paris was still Paris, and it still needed policing. By its own police. Even the swastika banner hanging from the roof did nothing to disrupt my resolve.

Nevin was alone in the aquarium, a cup of coffee going cold on the desk in front of him. He looked up as I entered.

'Thank God you're here,' he said, his eyes almost popping out of his thin pale face with anxiety, 'I hate being here alone. Philippe hasn't showed up yet, even the commissaire isn't in his office... What if the phone had rung?'

'You'd have answered it, you'd have listened calmly, you'd have noted down the essential details, you'd have initiated the correct procedures. It's all in the manuals, and you really are a perfectly competent detective, you know.'

'I'm not sure sometimes...'

'The boss not here yet, you say?'

I looked at the clock on the wall. This was unprecedented – Roland had the knack of somehow being everywhere before anyone else had dragged themselves from their beds.

'That German fellow been around over the weekend?' I asked.

'Not that I've seen, no.' Nevin was fidgeting with the items on his neat desktop, fussily rearranging them, obviously uncomfortable.

'Is there something you're wanting to say to me?'

He gulped, 'No.'

There had been just enough hesitation, just enough caution in the inflection of that 'No' to confirm that he was, indeed, struggling mightily within himself – something needed to be said, something that could not be said.

It came to me that I knew the source of young Nevin's acute discomfort. Perhaps because I disliked and distrusted him I had assumed that it was Clément who had been suborned into keeping Commissaire Six informed on the progress of our investigation, but now I knew better. Of course a vulnerable probationer was a more apt target for the machinations of an intelligence officer than a salty old pro like Clément, however corrupt. Clément would have demanded something in return, Nevin wouldn't know how to ask.

My Star Ruby automatic was on my desk along with a receipt that I was supposed to sign and return to the armoury. I sat, opened the drawer in which I kept a box of shells, and began to check and load my weapon while I thought about this. The phone rang and Nevin jumped and glared at me with the startled expression of a colt hearing a firecracker for the first time.

I answered, 'Saint-Simon,' observing with amusement Nevin's surprise out of the corner of my eye.

It was Meyer, the Director of the Service, the boss's boss. I listened. Clément came in, puffing out smoke like the Lyon express.

'Thank you, sir. I'll try to locate Hauptmann Jäger, see if he knows anything,' I said, hearing my own words as though spoken by someone at an immense distance. I replaced the phone gently in its cradle.

'The Germans have seized the boss along with four other commissaires of police,' I heard myself say and, as though to convince myself that I had heard my own words correctly: 'Commissaire Roland is under arrest and being held at an unknown location.'

46

It took me an hour to track Jäger down to a briefing at Palais Bourbon, and then I was told that I would have to wait a further forty minutes until he was free to call me back. But as soon as I hung up the telephone trilled. I picked up eagerly. It was Officer Peres, sounding as though he had contracted a bad case of the senile jitters, ringing from the station in the 4th.

'Is that you, Inspector Simon?' he quavered.

'I'll check. Yes, it's me, all right.'

There was a silence while he considered my reply and composed himself.

'It's Peres here, sir, 4th Arondissement. We have a report here, sir...' I waited. 'We... we're not sure what to do, sir...' He lapsed into a baffled silence.

'So you thought you'd better pass it up to the PJ?'

'That's right, sir, thank you, sir. See, we don't know what we can do, sir.'

The poor old fellow sounded out of his mind with worry and a hint of something else − indignation, I thought.

'Well, two heads are better than one. Tell me about it.'

'It' was an unsavoury incident from the previous night. A group of German soldiers had been drinking in a café on Rue de la Verrerie until the time came for the owner to announce that, in compliance with the 21.00 curfew, he was about to close. Most of the group finished their drinks, settled their bill and left, but two remained and demanded another bottle. When the patron refused, one lurched to the counter and angrily swept a dozen glasses and empty bottles to the floor, while the other remained seated but pulled his pistol from its holster and waved it in the air, firing several shots into the ceiling.

No one was injured by the gunshots but the drunk and incensed soldiers suddenly spotted the only other customer left in the café – a middle-aged Algerian, who was busy trying to shrink into invisibility in a corner – and decided to have some sport with him. They hauled the terrified man to his feet, roughed him up a little, demanded his ID, pretended to inspect the flimsy document and then set light to it in front of him. This entertainment concluded, one of them barged his way behind the counter and raided the till, pocketing the day's takings. At this point, one of their colleagues returned – possibly a non-commissioned officer – and dragged them out of the place with a shake of the head and muttered apologies to the patron.

I wasn't sure what to do either. From the other side of the aquarium Clément observed my struggle with an expression of sardonic satisfaction. Then the telephone on his desk rang.

'Do we know what unit these characters belonged to?' I asked Peres, playing for time and hoping vainly for some decisive plan of action to occur to me.

Under the law to which I had sworn my fidelity these men had committed a number of offences: criminal damage, endangering life and property by illegally discharging a firearm, assault and battery, theft, destruction of an official document, and probably others that did not come readily to mind. But how did the law apply to the soldiers of an occupying power? Like Peres, I felt baffled and indignant, and I sorely missed the Commissaire.

'The owner couldn't say,' I heard Peres reply. 'He said they wore field grey like most of them do...'

213

'All right,' I had decided on the only conceivable course of action, 'send the paperwork over to me and I'll follow it up.'

I replaced the receiver and looked over to where Clément had broken into a sweat in his desperate exertions to deflect the referral of some other matter to us.

'How many times do I have to fucking tell you?' he was saying. 'The PJ doesn't do bloody bike thefts.'

I could hear the voice at the other end of the line insisting ever more forcefully. I signalled to gain Clément's attention.

'German soldiers?' I guessed. He nodded gloomily, all of the complacency that had been aroused by my own dilemma extinguished. 'Tell them to send the paperwork to me,' I said to his transparent relief. This, I told myself, would be the Commissaire's response: take responsibility.

Before Jäger called back we fielded calls from stations across Paris – several incidents in which German soldiers had pulled people from their bicycles and made off with them, a couple in which troops had stolen cars, and one in which a gang of blue-shirted French youths had set about pillaging a Jewish-owned shop in the Marais, only to be stopped by the arrival of a German patrol. We noted them all and requested the written reports.

My telephone whirred once more. I regarded it with dislike, made it wait until, unable to bear its jangling clamour for attention any longer, I picked up. It was Jäger.

'You wished to speak to me, Inspector?'

Something snapped as soon as I heard that soft voice, that Swiss-scented French. It was as though some mechanism within had been wound up too tightly and, released, ran ineffectually amok – a child's toy, a tin dog

214 .

perhaps, yapping furiously as it spiralled around and ran into the wall.

He heard me out. Even as I ranted, venting fury, fear, humiliation, the image came to mind of him sitting at the other end of the line, the telephone held at a distance from his ear, those mild blue eyes popping in consternation behind the thick lenses, and the overwound mechanism within me stuttered, jammed and stilled, and all I had left to say was, 'Where is he? How could you?'

'Believe me, Joseph,' he said, 'I knew nothing of this. I am as surprised and distressed as you to hear of it.'

I believed him. I could hear the shock in his voice.

'Listen,' he said, 'We need to be careful until we know what is going on, so do nothing for now. I will find out what I can and call you back.'

It was late in the afternoon before he called again, and the flatness of his voice did not suggest that he had encouraging news.

'Inspector Saint-Simon please.'

'Speaking. Do you have anything?'

I was in no mood to speak his name, let alone acknowledge his military rank.

'Joseph, I am sorry to say that I have been unable to find out anything. I cannot even say which branch of the authorities have taken our friend and his colleagues into custody, nor where, nor why. I have made contact with your Prefect of Police and he was also unaware and is protesting in the strongest terms...'

'So what do we do now?' I cut him short.

'You and your colleagues can do nothing but continue your work. In fact, Monsieur Langeron has agreed to my suggestion that you should stand in as acting commissaire while Commissaire Roland is absent. You must trust me, Acting Commissaire, that I will continue to do all in my power to set him free.'

Acting Commissaire? I did not want it. In fact, the thought of stepping into Arthur Roland's shoes in these circumstances filled me with revulsion, but all I said was, 'What will you do now?'

I sensed his hesitation. He's a German, I thought, and he's not going to step on any superior's toes.

'I have been thinking... that I shall endeavour to contact SS-Obergruppenführer Heydrich himself. He knows me, he will remember me... I am almost certain he will take my call, and I do know that he is a great admirer of Commissaire Roland...'

Despite myself, I was impressed. Jäger was declaring himself willing to play one arm of the German state against another for the sake of his one-time colleague. I realised that this could go dreadfully wrong for him.

'I wish you luck with it,' I said and, feeling more at ease with him, 'There is one more thing, while I have you, Hauptmann Jäger.' I told him about the reports of German petty crime that had been coming in all morning from local stations across Paris.

'This conduct is unworthy of soldiers of the German army,' he said. 'One of the cars belonged to a doctor, you say? How is he to do his house calls? Send me the reports and I shall see to it that this behaviour is stopped at once and the perpetrators punished. The doctor will have his car back by the morning.'

47

When I arrived at work the next morning I found Madame Roland waiting on the chair outside her husband's office. She rose to her feet as I approached to shake her hand, and took me by surprise by enfolding me in a warm embrace and then holding me at arm's length and gazing steadily into my eyes. Her eyes were grey-green with bright golden sparks that flashed in the light, her brown hair was cut shorter than I remembered, her face a pale oval, unlined despite her nearly fifty years. She was tall for a woman and met me eye to eye.

'We must be brave, Joseph,' she said, fixing me with her eyes to emphasise the point. 'There will be many trials ahead.'

I thought of her son, Sébastien, away at the front like my brother. Were they alive or dead, free or taken prisoner?

'How is Annette?' Her daughter was studying law at the Sorbonne.

'The universities and schools are closed, so she is at home with me all day, with nothing to do but wait for news. But she is strong.'

'She's her father's and mother's daughter – how could she not be strong? Shall we?'

I opened the door to the commissaire's office – temporarily my office – and invited her to enter.

She unbuttoned the jacket of her dove grey suit as she sat down on one of the plywood chairs. Beneath it she wore a plain white blouse open at the throat, a strand of pearls around her neck. I took the other suspects' chair and sat in front of her, trying not to evade eye contact.

'What have you heard, Joseph?'

I sighed, 'In effect, nothing, madame.'

'Héloïse. Remember?'

'Of course. We know that your husband and four other commissaires were taken into custody, but we have no idea why they were arrested and others were not.'

She nodded gravely.

'We don't yet know where they are, or even who exactly has taken them. The Germans seem to have various strands of authority running in parallel without much communication between them.'

Explaining the situation to her was helping me to understand more clearly the nature of the creature into whose grasp we had fallen.

'A liaison officer, if that's what he is, from the German military police has been attached to us...'

She nodded, 'Walther Jäger – Arthur knew him before the war.'

'Yes, well, he seems to be trying to help. He's trying to get in touch with the overall head of security to have Commissaire Roland released. It seems this man has also met the commissaire in person.'

'That would be Heydrich? Arthur told me about meeting him. He sounds an absolutely monstrous specimen. Why would he care enough to help?'

Given her words, her composure was nothing short of magnificent.

Mine was not. I felt a pit of despair opening within and was suddenly struggling to hold back tears. I shook my head, 'I don't know, but it has to be worth trying. Jäger insists that Heydrich held your husband in very high regard.'

'Monsieur Langeron, the Prefect of Police, called yesterday and again this morning, which was good of him,' she said. 'Even he is in the dark, though I do trust him to do everything to press for the release of his men, even if it costs him his career. I do hope he's not arrested too.'

'Indeed – let's hope it doesn't come to that.'

We sat in silence for a while, each of us nursing our burden of grief and foreboding until, flushing with shame, I recognised my unforgivable lapse of courtesy and jumped to my feet.

'Coffee, madame, you must have coffee... or tea perhaps?'

She rose and placed a consoling hand on my elbow.

'I won't, Joseph, thank you. I must go home now and leave you to your work. You know where I am when you have news.'

She paused in the doorway and nodded towards the commissaire's old leather chair.

'You must keep Arthur's chair warm for him while he's away, Joseph – no one better.'

And then she was gone, leaving behind her a waft of fragrance like the fading memory of elegance.

48

That week time flowed with the viscid reluctance of spilt molasses. Outside the narrow confines of home and office to which I restricted myself as I continued my frantic quest for news of Commissaire Roland, life was slowly returning to the city. Thanks to Langeron's astute centralisation of supplies, shops and restaurants were able to open for business, including our favourite in Place Dauphine. Refugees were beginning to trickle back to or through Paris and, one by one, the schools re-opened. The German army trumpeted in triumph along the Champs Élysées each day and the streets thronged with field grey but, try as I might, I could not locate Hauptmann Jäger, who seemed increasingly to be our only hope.

Meanwhile, two radio broadcasts at the beginning of the week sparked bitter, exhausting arguments between long-time friends and colleagues. Our new head of state, Marshall Pétain, the hero of Verdun no less, declared to the nation that it was time for the fighting to stop. Taking him at his word, at least a million French troops immediately laid down their arms and were promptly taken prisoner.

The very next evening, far fewer people heard – but everyone soon heard about – a broadcast from London. An obscure French officer named de Gaulle invoked 'the flame of French resistance' and called upon the nation to fight on. But what, some wondered, could 'resistance' mean in our present plight?

The Occupation of Paris was to prove the most crime-ridden period of the modern era, but I could not know that and there was little foreshadowing of things to come in that first week. There were crimes and disturbing events, to be sure – sixteen suicides were reported, a few Jewish businesses suffered harassment, a number of abandoned homes were burgled, and an attempted raid on a food stockpile at Les Halles was foiled by alert gardiens de la paix. But otherwise a sombre stillness prevailed, as though the city and its people were mourning the violent death of the Republic and waiting uneasily to learn what was to succeed it.

Early on Thursday morning I received a call from a most unexpected source: Claude Rospeau.

'That guy you were asking about – Niki, the Russian? Mate of Tom Pouce?'

'I remember.'

'Well, he booked into my hotel with a tart last night. Should still be there if you're interested.'

I thought of the unsolved mystery of who had set the watchers onto us.

'Oh, I'm interested. But why are you telling me?'

'Well, new world isn't it? I scratch your back, maybe one day you'll scratch mine.' He rang off before I could frame a reply.

I gathered up Nevin and a deeply resentful Clément and we headed straight over to Passage Thiéré in the Traction Avant, Clément in the driver's seat with Nevin beside him, which obliged me to take the back seat despite my reluctance to flaunt my temporary elevation.

We travelled in silence through the quiet streets until Clément, evidently able to contain himself no longer, caught my eye in the mirror and sneered, 'Best mates with that German cunt are you, Simon?'

He paused to permit the shock to register. The backs of Nevin's ears had turned scarlet with embarrassment.

'I don't know why I'm surprised,' Clément continued, 'your lot always does know whose arse to lick. I don't reckon it'll do you much good for long, though – not when they get really fucking started, so watch out.'

221

Struggling to suppress the rage that swelled within me, I managed to confine myself to, 'What do you mean by my lot?'

'Israélites. Who did you think I meant?'

Rage collapsed into something approaching terror, as though I had been flushed from some secure place of refuge into the jaws of the pack. I found that I was trembling but, to my own surprise, defiant.

'What the fuck makes you think I'm Jewish?' I said. 'Because I can fucking well read? Molière was a fucking Yid too, was he, if you've ever heard of him?'

I was glad that the two in front could not get a clear sight of me, toiling in the grip of powerfully conflicting emotions. Nevin's shoulders were shaking and I realised that he was laughing.

'Ha!' he said tentatively. 'See, I told you, Philippe.'

I could sense Clément's scowl from the set of his head.

'You can shut the fuck up, too, Nevin,' he said. 'Cheeky cunt.'

'Just drive, Clément,' I said, injecting a note of weary irritation into my voice, my mouth so dry that it was an effort to speak at all.

He shrugged and drove with increased vehemence. At Place de la Bastille the German army had set up machine gun posts and roadblocks, and Clément brought the Traction Avant to a grudging halt. A fresh-faced soldier courteously inspected our warrant cards and went off to consult his officer, who came to make his own inquiries. Clément indicated with a jerk of the thumb that he should address himself to me.

'Police Judiciaire? What is this?'

The officer's French was clearly inadequate to cope with this conversation and I had no Hochdeutsch so I chanced my arm.

'Would you be more comfortable if we spoke English, perhaps?' I ventured.

A fleeting smile, quickly suppressed, of gratitude.

'Indeed I would. Your English is excellent, by the way.'

This young fellow, tall, lean and earnest, seemed unable to conceal his essential decency for more than a few moments.

'Thank you. Yours too.'

Clément sat glowering and Nevin open-mouthed as this bizarre and incomprehensible dialogue continued over their heads.

'The Police Judiciaire is the investigative branch – detectives, you know, CID in English,' I explained. 'We're on a case and we need to get across to Passage Thiéré urgently, to interview a suspect before he disappears again.'

An eager look that I recognised only too well entered his eyes – a fellow devotee of detective literature. He nodded knowingly and passed our warrant cards through the open window.

'Of course, we are not here to prevent the Paris CID from carrying out its duty. Richter here,' he indicated the young soldier who had stopped us, 'will ride with you to see you through the checkpoint on the other side. Good luck.' He was about to step back but instead leaned forward again to speak confidentially, 'What has he done, this suspect?'

'That,' I said, 'is what we are trying to find out.'

'Of course,' he said, smiling in satisfaction with my professional discretion – just like the terse detectives in magazines and films. 'Of course it is.'

Giving a little bow, he waved us on.

49

The interior of the Quatre Saisons hotel was exactly as I had imagined it – dark and distressed. The walls were peeling, the ceiling was speckled with mould and the rust-brown stains of historic leaks, and the tiled floor in Reception was liberally littered with cigarette butts and old lottery tickets. This was a place where shattered dreams came to die.

The reek of stale cigarette smoke hung everywhere about the place and, beneath that, the clammy odour of damp rot. An insistent press of the button on the unmanned reception desk set off an unearthly rattling sound, the dry wings of innumerable locusts, somewhere in the distance, but nobody came.

'Niki' was still in bed in the fourth room we tried, his companion of the previous night long gone. The air in the stifling little room conveyed a uriniferous tang from the half-filled chamberpot beneath the bed. Daylight peeked through holes in the blind but there was nothing to see but the bed and its rumpled, greasy sheets, a wooden chair and an unseemly bundle of clothes on the floor. It was as though we had accidentally stumbled into the den of some wild beast. The Russian was still snoring. So much for operational readiness.

Clément seized him by the shoulders and hauled him, startled, from his bed. He was naked, his penis retracting in fright to peer out from its thicket of wiry red hair. He was a powerfully-built man and he struggled to escape Clément's expert hold at first but, once he had registered that there were three of us, he became still and watchful.

'What the fuck you want, hey? You got wrong man here,' he protested.

I signalled to Nevin to open the blind and, as light felt its way cautiously around the walls, he looked at me with recognition. Blood, still bright, filled the white of the right eye.

'I know you, hey?' he said contemptuously. 'You are policeman. What you want with me, hey? You got nothing on me.'

Following a brief visual inspection of its surface, I sat on the chair, crossing my legs and withdrawing a cigarette from the pack in my pocket. Clément dropped his prisoner onto the bed, where he sat rubbing the back of his head and watching me in silent hostility.

'I should think you do know me,' I said, 'since you were watching my apartment so closely.' I lit my cigarette and held the pack out to him, offering.

He shook his head: 'So I stand in street. Is not crime.'

He was thinking now, I could see it, wondering if we had anything else.

'Why run when I challenged you then?'

He smirked, 'You have gun pointing at me, what am I going to do?'

I nodded slowly: 'Then there's the girl, the young woman you ambushed on the stairs in her building. That was you, wasn't it Niki? That nice splash of scarlet in your eye tells me so.'

He was shaking his head, his brow furrowed in feigned perplexity.

'Don't bother to deny it, Niki, we've obtained your fingerprint records from the Legion and we've lifted your dabs from four places in that building.'

Nevin, who had been watching the suspect's face, looked up in surprise.

Now the Russian was trying to remember what he had touched, whether he had wiped everything;

225

whether, indeed, the Legion had ever taken his fingerprints.

'So,' he said, 'Maybe I go to visit friend there – what place, what address?'

'Give it up, Niki, she identified you. She'd served you at the bar, remember? Putting out all the lights, grabbing a girl from behind, threatening her... I reckon that amounts to attempted rape, that does.'

'That is shit.' But he wasn't sure. Time to put the screws on.

'You worked with Thomas Fabricant, didn't you, Niki?'

He couldn't deny it. He nodded. Looking me in the eye, he made a smoking gesture with his right hand. I handed him a cigarette and signalled to Clément to light it for him.

'And then you killed him.'

He was up on his feet. Clément punched him in the head, launching his cigarette in an arc that grounded beneath my chair, and hauled him back onto the bed. Dazed, he sat heavily and Clément swiftly applied the handcuffs behind his back. I ground the cigarette out under my foot, staring pointedly into the Russian's eyes.

'It's the guillotine for you, Niki.'

'That is shit, shit. I was looking for him.'

'He's dead. You killed him.'

'No. This is shit.'

'Yes. The Comte de l'Île gave the order and you carried it out.'

'No. Count told me find him, find my best boy, Niki. I don't give shit about fucking Count but I swear he never knows Tommy is dead neither. He wants him back, his best fucking boy, hey?'

So it was the Chevaliers. But as one door opened another slammed shut. The watch was put on us only after we had informed the Count of the supposed

226

murder of his supposed henchman. He knew he was dead so why order a search for him?

'The Comte de l'Île knew very well that Tommy was dead, Niki. I was there when he heard the news. So you're going to have to do better than that.' I turned to Nevin, 'Search the room, go through his clothes and belongings – everything.'

Nevin nodded and set eagerly to work, beginning with the clothes heaped on the floor. Our captive sat on the bed, hands on his knees, apparently unconcerned by his nakedness. His stillness suggested that he was beginning to compose himself, to think more clearly.

Items began to accumulate on the bed beside him as Nevin's search proceeded: a wallet, a tobacco pouch, a pack of cigarette papers, a book of matches from Chez Maurice, a joint in rue de Lappe, a keyring with a single key attached, a handful of small change, a carnet of Métro tickets (second class), and a lead-weighted cosh and a flick-knife.

'Full name?' I demanded.

'Nikolai Denisovich Volkov,' he replied without hesitation.

Nevin, who was perusing his identity card, nodded.

'Date and place of birth?'

'30 January 1904; Arkhangelsk, USSR.'

Nevin nodded.

'Why did you leave Mother Russia, Nikolai?'

'Too cold up there.'

'Try again.'

'Too many flies in summer.'

I gave Clément a look and then looked quickly away. I heard a sharp expulsion of breath and when I looked again the Russian was grimacing with pain and resisting the impulse to wipe away the tears that a swift punch in the kidneys brings involuntarily to the eyes.

'Again?'

'All right. I was starving there, is that what you want to hear?'

Despite his rough treatment his expression seemed strangely free of hate. Rather, I felt that he was calculating the effect of his words, observing us.

'I come to the West, to France, to try for a better life. Some hope!'

'So you signed up for the Foreign Legion?'

He shrugged, 'At least they feed you.'

I picked up the tobacco pouch and began to rifle through it – nothing but thick strands of pungent black tobacco.

'What the hell is this muck?' I asked.

'Is Russian – reminds me of home. Can I?' He eyed the tobacco hungrily.

'Wait.'

I examined the little packet of papers, pulled one or two out: nothing. I gestured to Clément to remove the handcuffs and handed the tobacco and papers to the Russian. I watched him as he moistened and tore off the edge of the paper, filled it with a pinch of tobacco and a tightly rolled tube of card torn from the book of matches, and began to roll – a precise operation, calling for steady hands.

'Did you know Tommy in the Legion?' I asked.

He inhaled deeply. Oily plumes of smoke coiled through the room, the aroma that of a conflagration in a stable that has somehow spread to a perfume manufactory.

'Sure, I knew Tommy. He was a legend – best boy in Legion too.'

There was no trace of envy or resentment in his voice or expression.

'How did you come to be working for the Chevaliers de la France Catholique, Nikolai?'

He was watching Nevin now, as he picked up each item of clothing and ran his fingers meticulously along every seam.

'I don't know... Tommy introduce me maybe.'

'Well, did he or didn't he?' I too was watching Nevin with half an eye.

'Yes,' he said distractedly, 'That's how it was. Tommy say come along, Niki, good money to be made for a tough guy like you... Hey, careful with that – is my only one.'

Nevin had gathered up the flick-knife and was carefully unpicking the seam in the armpit of his suit jacket. Clément gripped the Russian's head and forced him to turn his gaze on me.

'Never mind what he's doing, look at me,' I said, nodding to Clément. 'And your story is that, despite having been formally informed by the Police Judiciaire that Thomas Fabricant was dead, the Count ordered you to go looking for him.'

'Sure, he don't believe what he don't want to believe, and he don't believe there's a man been born could get better of his best boy.'

He was desperate to see what Nevin was up to, but Clément kept his gaze locked on me.

'He say, you go, Niki, find his girl, watch those police bastards, take who you need, bring Tommy back to me.' He was sweating now. 'Now I think it, I reckon that old Count, he was a little bit queer for Tommy, know what I'm saying?'

'Look at this, boss,' Nevin said quietly.

Clément grunted and suddenly released his grip on the Russian's head, and all eyes were on the young detective and the sliver of paper that he held between two fingers.

50

Volkov, if that was his name, relaxed, leaning back on the bed and enjoying the last of his smoke. Clément maintained his vigil over the contented smoker while Nevin and I examined the flimsy document that he had just discovered. It was a cigarette paper on which someone had inscribed a list of numbers in pencil: six groups of five. I held it up for our prisoner to see.
'What is this?'

He shrugged and stubbed his cigarette out on the floor. 'Something to do with the tailor?' he suggested. 'Can I get dressed now, if you have finished with them?'

He indicated the neatly folded pile of clothes where Nevin had left them at the foot of the bed.

'In a minute. Who else do you work for, Nikolai?'

It was obvious to me that the concealed paper contained some form of encrypted information to be consulted only in an emergency.

'Who?'

He shook his head, 'I don't know what you're talking about. I never seen that before, it means nothing to me.'

'What is it? A telephone number, the address of a safe house?'

Not a flicker of reaction, just the steady gaze of a professional about his business.

'Who are you, Niki? Just who am I speaking to here? Are you an officer of the NKVD?'

At my suggestion that he might work for Soviet intelligence, he pursed his lips and tilted his head to one side in a manner that might almost have been described as coquettish.

'That is ridiculous. But you do realise that if I were an NKVD operative,' his French had suddenly increased in fluency and acquired a subjunctive mood, 'you would currently be mistreating an official of a state closely allied to the occupying power. Awkward, hey? But never mind, I am not.'

'And neither are you simply a loyal foot soldier in the service of the Count.'

He raised an eyebrow and glanced in the direction of his clothes.

'All right, get dressed, we're done with you,' I said, wondering quite how widely and deeply the Count's organisation was penetrated.

I found myself smirking at the fantasy that the secret army which that vain, pompous old aristocrat had dreamed of leading into battle against the Republic was nothing other than a regiment of secret agents in the service of his enemies. Suddenly I remembered a book I had read years ago; an English novel, by Chesterton.

Volkov was already fully dressed and now, under the glowering gaze of Clément, was dispersing his belongings about his person. He looked up and smiled at me.

'No hard feeling, Inspector,' he said, offering a hand for me to shake, 'but time I go.'

His command of French syntax had deteriorated markedly with the donning of his cheap suit. He assumed a convincingly mournful expression as he fingered the hole that Nevin had opened in the armpit.

'I bill PJ for repair.'

We laughed.

I accompanied him to the door and stepped into the gloomy corridor with him, closing the door behind us. Detaining him a moment with a hand on his sleeve, I drew close and spoke in a near-whisper.

'None of us can know how things are going to turn out,' I said, 'but I doubt your country's alliance with Germany will last. Let there be a code-word between us

– Thursday. And, should our interests ever coincide, I'll place a small ad in the window of the Tabac du Marché on rue Mouffetard. The word 'Thursday' will be in it somewhere. When you've seen it, have it taken down, and I'll meet you the next Tuesday night at ten in the place you got that matchbook from.'

He gave me a quizzical look then nodded and turned to leave.

'Thursday,' I reminded him, 'Remember Thursday.'

Only after he had gone did I remember that today was Thursday.

51

Friday began badly for me. I was getting ready to go to work – the pale linen suit that Ammarah said made her think of ice cream, white shirt, blue silk tie, topped off with my father's Panama – when there was a knock at the door.

Ammarah, still dripping from the bath, wrapped my dressing gown around herself and ran to answer it. I heard the door open, a murmur of conversation, and then a squeal of delight followed by the door closing. When I emerged into the hall, I found her clinging to Pino Zagaria as though he had just saved her from drowning. I hoped that the dressing gown hadn't slipped open.

'Oh, darling, Pino has come to tell me that we re-open tonight! Isn't that wonderful?' she beamed.

The gloom I felt was instant and profound, and I saw that it was in danger of clouding her delight.

'Marvellous,' I said unconvincingly and, to Pino, 'Now that you're one of our conquerors, I suppose you can do as you please.'

I had intended it as a light satirical quip but, even to my own ears, the tone sounded wrong – bitter, defensive.

Pino tried his best to look hurt, his bottom lip jutting comically as though he might burst into tears.

'No, no, it is nothing like that, I swear it. The word's gone out, the Germans want Paris back to normal, everything back to normal, so they want places to open again...'

The oiled hair, the freshly-shaved face, the bottle-green suit with a red carnation at the lapel, and the white patent leather shoes were an emphatic declaration that Pino was back in business. He smiled broadly and I couldn't help feeling pleased for him – he wasn't altogether a bad sort.

'Normal, eh?' I said, planting my father's hat on my head. 'Well, I'm just off to work, as normal, so I'll see you out, Monsieur Zagaria.'

We left Ammarah poised between pouting in annoyance at my attitude and laughing with joy at the resumption of her life of music, lights, and the admiration of strangers.

Alone in Roland's office, I stood at the window and stared unseeing over the city. The whirr of the telephone shook me from my self-pitying reverie.

'Commissaire Roland?'

I recognised the dry, rustling voice of juge d'instruction Leclerc, like autumn leaves underfoot. This was all I needed.

'Inspector Simon speaking.' A slip – I needed to get used to my new, expanded name, quickly. 'I am afraid Commissaire Roland is not here, Monsieur. The Germans...'

'Never mind. You'll have to do, Simon, I have little time.'

'You're in Paris, Monsieur?'

'I arrived this morning with the governmental delegation.'

He left that hanging in the void between us, letting it be known that he could say no more about it. He had told me just enough to hint at his vertiginous standing, while reminding me that I was too lowly to be entrusted with high confidences.

I understood immediately, however, that he and his colleagues must be here to negotiate France's capitulation. Thoroughly dispirited yet passively defiant, I said nothing and waited for him to break the silence.

'The case of the man murdered on the Métro,' he said. 'I issued a Commission Rogatoire to Roland...'

So he was anxious about that – abdicating his judicial authority and handing it down to common police officers while he fled his post in Paris. From Roland's high window I could see a group of boys on the towpath on the Left Bank, throwing stones at a duck and her brood. I waited in silence, forcing Leclerc to ask for what he wanted.

'You will update me on the progress of the case, Simon.'

'It's over, monsieur,' I said, wishing I were close enough to tell those little ruffians to stop, to ask them what they thought they were doing, to shame them so that they would never perpetrate such barbarism again.

The door opened and closed at my back but I disregarded it, concentrated on willing an end to the boys' cruelty and Leclerc's arrogance. Nevin and his latest message could wait.

'Come, Simon, I shall require more than that, man.'

The duck had gathered her brood and shepherded them out of the range of the boys' wayward artillery. Thwarted, the little shits moved on, pushing and shoving, joyful in the sunlit morning. I expected their school would soon re-open, putting an end to their short-lived freedom. I sighed loudly.

'What's that? How dare you sigh at me...'

'Would you like some help with that, Jojo?'

His voice. Him! Overcome, I span round to verify the evidence of my ears. He reached to take the telephone from my nerveless fingers.

'Roland here... Yes, monsieur, that is correct, the case is closed... The perpetrator took his own life... No, monsieur, there is no doubt... Thank you, and good luck in the talks... Yes, they told me this morning... Goodbye, Monsieur le Juge.'

He smiled at me as I stood there, open-mouthed and momentarily speechless. He appeared dishevelled and unlaundered but his reassuring bulk, his solidity and imperturbability were undiminished.

'Don't that suit show the dirt, Jojo?' he said, casting a dubious glance at my cream linen outfit.

'Welcome back,' I said, 'I am so glad to see you, boss.'

'I think I'd better call my wife,' he said, easing himself down into his chair, snatching up the telephone and rattling furiously at the switch hook to alert the operator.

52

They had come for him in the night, he told me. Two men in leather trench-coats with hats pulled down to shade their eyes – 'Like they'd watched too many American crime films' – accompanied by a grim-faced soldier toting a submachine gun.

They had knocked, politely but insistently, on the door and had waited while he threw some clothes on, but would not allow him to take a bag of any kind. They would not, or could not, provide any explanation for his arrest and treated his demand to see their IDs and authorisation with silent contempt. As to Roland's request that he be allowed to telephone his superior, the reply was a terse, 'What makes you think there's anyone left to take your call?'

Roland asked that he be permitted to comfort his wife and daughter and bid them a dignified farewell, but this too was denied.

'Please to stay in your rooms, ladies. No harm will come,' said the same plainclothesman.

'I had the impression he was the only one of them who spoke any French,' said Roland.

We were waiting to be served in the restaurant around the corner in Place Dauphine, which had re-opened without explanation, as though nothing untoward had occurred.

As he was marched down the stairs in handcuffs, Roland looked back, hoping for a last glimpse of Héloïse but the door had closed on her. He was, however, able to check the insignia on the infantryman's uniform.

'No insignia. Nothing.' he said. 'Not good.'

'No insignia? So no accountability. That's disturbing,' I said, thinking aloud.

'It tells you all you need to know about these people. We can't trust that we're operating and living under the rule of law. I saw what that meant in Germany...'

Outside on the street, a black van had been waiting, engine throbbing. Roland was conducted to the back of the van and required to climb in. Inside, a bench ran along each side, a rail above. One of the faux detectives chained Roland to the rail, signalled that he should sit, and left.

The door slammed shut and Roland was in darkness. He suddenly remembered something Heydrich had said to him on the occasion of their dinner engagement. It was a recommendation regarding police procedure.

'Take them by night and by fog,' he had said.

I experienced a sudden somatic sensation of extreme coldness.

'He actually called it "police procedure"? Kidnapping, more like.'

Roland nodded, his expression more openly troubled than I had ever known it. I needed to move on and put the image of people snatched 'by night and by fog' behind me.

'Where did they take you?'

'They wouldn't tell me where we were going. We drove for about twenty minutes, then I was hooded and they handed me down into the street. I heard the door in front of us being unlocked – a big door, plenty of locks and bolts – and I knew straightaway that they'd brought me to a prison. I knew we were still in Paris – that was a city sidewalk beneath my feet – and I reckoned we'd crossed the river, so I knew I'd been taken to a prison on the Left Bank. The place was completely silent, eerie, like no prison has ever been at night, so I knew it was empty. And which prison had been evacuated before the enemy entered Paris?'

'The military gaol – Prison du Cherche-Midi.'

'Exactly – it had to be Cherche-Midi. They hustled me up two flights of stairs and into a cell – no formalities, no admission process at all – and then they removed the hood and cuffs, took my wristwatch away and left me.'

He sat on the bed and looked around the cell. He had visited this prison once or twice in the pursuit of inquiries, and knew that prisoners were customarily held in solitary confinement. His cell – for whatever period his detention here continued – conformed to that pattern: bed, table, chair, bucket.

The window had been blacked out but the early morning sounds reaching him from below – the rattle of a handcart on cobbles, the clatter of shutters being opened – suggested that he was in a cell overlooking the street. The electric light in the ceiling was on and, it seemed to him, brighter than would be normal in a prison cell. This light would not be extinguished, day or night, for the duration of his detention.

He laid himself down on the bed and waited. After an indeterminate number of hours, he heard the jangle of keys, the hefty click of the lock, and the door opened just enough to allow unseen hands to push a tin tray bearing a hunk of bread and an enamel jug of water into the room. After that he was left alone until, he estimated, noon.

He knew nothing, at first, of the detention of the other commissaires, but he heard voices once or twice and, on one occasion, a voice raised in angry protest. It was unmistakably that of Farinet, Commissaire of the Montsouris division, so then he knew that he was not alone.

'Did you manage to speak to any of the others?'

I did not yet know that only he had been released and returned to duty.

He shook his head, 'No. They kept me in complete isolation. Have they taken all of the commissaires, do you know?'

Only then did I pause to wonder at the sheer capriciousness of the whole affair.

'Just you and four others. It seems odd, doesn't it – just the five of you? I mean, why you five and not the others? No offence, but what's special about you? It's bizarre. What did they want with you?'

'Do you know, I have no idea. They came for me around noon that first day and at random times after that – day or night, sometimes twice in an hour, sometimes leaving me to stew for what felt like a whole day – and took me down to an interrogation room. Two men in suits there to interrogate me – menacing, but no rough stuff.

'The thing is that there was no real direction to their questioning, no strong feeling that they wanted anything at all. Most of the time they wanted to talk about my politics and my feelings about Germany and the Germans, and there's not much to discuss there.

'Look, I said in the end, you want to know about my politics, I'm a Frenchman, have a look at any French coin and see what it says there – "Liberty, Equality, Fraternity" – and that's it, that's my politics and that's how I feel about people, Germans and all.

'In the end I got the impression that they weren't much interested, that the whole exercise was connected to some kind of internal rivalry, just to make a point – one lot showing the others (and us, by the way) that they could do this, whenever they wanted.'

I don't remember what we had to eat that lunchtime, but I know we ate it in silence as we contemplated all this and the darkness of the new dawn it heralded. After the waiter had left our coffee Roland surprised me by requesting a cigarette.

240

'You'll lose your puff,' I reminded him as I leaned forward to light it, and he smiled for the first time. The smile died rapidly away as he smoked and lapsed again into thought.

'Another thing I don't begin to understand,' he said, 'is why I was suddenly released and not the others. I refused to leave without my comrades but they just cuffed me, hooded me, put me back in the van and dropped me on the doorstep of 36.'

'They haven't released the others?'

'No. Well, not as far as I know.'

It was slow in coming, but I realised that I probably had the answer.

'Jäger!' I said. 'Jäger said he was going to try to contact Heydrich about you. I haven't been able to track him down since – he's nowhere to be found – but he must have managed it. I think Heydrich must have ordered your release.'

'Fuck that!' he said. That was it, the only time I ever heard him curse.

53

Nevin intercepted us on the stairs as we were returning from lunch, and his expressive face told me that he brought only bad news.

'He's in there now, having our office cleared out, boss... Says he's going to have it... I didn't know what to... I saw you coming to the main door, so I ducked out for a moment to let you know... He's even got us cleaning the windows... Clément's furious and... I didn't know what to do,' he finished lamely.

'Calm down, lad, take a breath,' said Roland, placing a fatherly hand on the young man's shoulder. 'Who's doing this? Jäger? Doesn't sound much like him.'

Nevin was shaking his head so vigorously that I worried he might be overtaken by vertigo and take a tumble down the stairs.

'No, monsieur le commissaire, not Hauptmann Jäger. Someone new.'

Roland gave me a look and then, wearily rubbing the back of his neck, spoke quietly and reassuringly to poor Nevin, who seemed beside himself with nerves.

'Well, let's go and have a look, shall we? See what's going on here.'

The furniture had, indeed, been removed from the aquarium and was stacked untidily in the corridor, leaving barely sufficient space to squeeze past. Clément was unenthusiastically attacking the smoke-bronzed windows with a damp cloth, half a bucket of soapy water at his feet, and a dark scowl on his face which became positively venomous as soon as he spotted the return of Nevin.

In the centre of the room an erect figure in a field grey tunic with a green collar, jodhpurs and gleaming riding boots stood with his back to us, apparently taking detailed notes in a leather-bound pocket book. Behind me, Nevin whispered something but I was watching from the doorway as Roland advanced upon the intruder, jaw jutting like the prow of a battleship steaming into action.

'Commissaire Arthur Roland,' he barked. 'Who are you?'

Languidly, the stranger raised a single manicured finger and then continued to take his note. This completed, he snapped the book shut, pocketed it, and turned his head to meet Roland's boiling gaze.

The two men were of a height, but there any resemblance ended. Our unwanted visitor was trim, almost frail in figure and, when he had removed his braided cap, presented the profile of a poet. Golden hair fell in a crescent over his high brow, transparent lashes glittered in the dusty sunlight, and full, sensitive lips parted as he finally acknowledged the presence of the commissaire.

'We shall speak in your office, Commissaire,' said the German in faultless French.

I saw now that he was a man of about my own age, though with the self-assured bearing of one more senior and the features of a youthful Adonis. Observation had brought me to the conclusion that the Wehrmacht had purposely left the most handsome and mannerly among its soldiers to occupy Paris and charm its population into complaisance, and this man surely represented the apogee of this strategy of seduction. The bastard was beautiful, a nonpareil.

'All right, but my deputy, Inspector Saint-Simon, should also be there,' said Roland.

So, I was his deputy now. I could feel the fierce red heat of Clément's resentment radiating across the room.

'As you wish. Kindly show the way.'

243

Roland held the door open and the German officer preceded him into the office and occupied the chair behind the desk, delicately brushing his riding breeches to avoid the appearance of creases. A look passed between Roland and me, and we took the little chairs reserved for suspects and witnesses.

'Good,' said the German with a cold smile which went nowhere near his ice-blue eyes. 'You may retain your office, Commissaire. I prefer one which enables me to see all that is going on in the department.'

He seemed to be implying that Roland had been somehow negligent in not keeping a constant watch on his officers. A sidelong glance confirmed that Roland had not missed the insult.

But, 'I don't understand,' was his mild response. 'Hauptmann Jäger of the Feldgendarmerie is the liaison officer to the PJ. I'll need to speak to him about this.'

'Jäger has been reassigned and the supervision of the Police Judiciaire will be my remit from today. I am SS-Obersturmführer Albrecht Winter, seconded to the Geheime Feldpolizei, and you will report to me.'

'Supervision! Report! This is not what the Prefect of Police agreed with your authorities. We are to be allowed to conduct our work as civilian police officers without such obstacles, that was the clear and firm agreement.'

Roland's face was red with anger, a blood vessel on his temple throbbed.

'With the military authorities, yes.' The perfectly manicured fingers steepled beneath the perfect chin. 'There is, however, a political dimension. The decision has been taken, and that is it. The Geheime Feldpolizei and, in due course, the Geheime Staatspolizei will assume responsibility for the supervision of the Police Judiciaire. Furniture for my office will be requisitioned elsewhere and will arrive this evening.'

244

'The Gestapo, you say?' Somehow, Roland remained in control of his rage and continued in a firm but even voice, 'I will consult Monsieur Langeron, the Prefect of Police, about this.'

'The Prefect of Police has been removed and confined to his home until a decision has been taken about his future in the role. You may not contact him until such a decision has been made. You may proceed with your duties in the normal way.'

He broke off, his perfect nose wrinkled in disgust.

'What is that disgusting smell everywhere?'

'That is Paris, Monsieur,' Roland replied. 'For the time being, that stink is all yours.'

Winter stared at him, searching the commissaire's inscrutable face for evidence of ridicule. Finding none, he stood and walked – rather stiffly in the absurd riding breeches – the few steps to the door. There he turned, like a man in possession of an afterthought or a live grenade. He threw it into the room.

'Tomorrow morning you will provide me with a comprehensive list of Jewish officers and officials in the Police Judiciaire. Send it to me at the Hôtel du Louvre, first thing.'

And he walked out.

When I was a boy, I liked to look up at the night sky from the roof of our building and try to identify stars and planets and constellations. I assumed I was seeing all that was there to see, but my father would say, 'Ah, but the City of Light conceals the true nature of things from us. Just wait until you look out into the galaxy from a peak in the Massif Central. Then you will see, then you will understand.'

Of course, I dismissed his words. Then, one year, we took a rare family holiday to the Massif Central, and on a clear night I stood beside my father on a high plateau and we looked up and out into the infinite fecundity of the universe.

An unimaginable profusion of stars, of other worlds, spread like an opalescent membrane across the endless sky. It was as though I had peered through the dark, coarse weave of my understanding and perceived, in pin-points, the eternal, blazing light of a wondrous reality beyond. It was an epiphany. I had thought I knew everything, but I had known nothing. I was nothing.

My father laid a consoling arm across my shoulders and whispered, 'Now do you see?'

Roland was looking at me, tenderness in his eyes. As darkness seemed about to envelop my being, I knew what he was going to say.

THE END

By the same author,

'The Dying of the Fire', a novel of 1558.